How I Discovered That I Am A Genius

The Satirical Memoir

of A Madman

JEREMY JUDE

DEDICATION

I want to dedicate this memoir to my sister Candice and her foreign husband Leo, to my mother Merilyn and my lawyer father Edward, to Lana Allen, and most importantly, to my fellow geniuses who are unfairly scrutinized by society as well. Hang in there!

CONTENTS

ACKNOWLEDGMENTS

I want to thank my editor Jennifer Phillips for her incredible work ethic and great insights. Jen, thanks for suggesting the full re-write of chapter 12. It was hard to hear, but well worth it in the end.

I also want to thank my family and friends for listening to me read entire chapters out-loud in the early stages. Your laughter confirmed my jokes to be humorous, and your awkward silences made me painfully aware when it was time for a rewrite.

CHAPTER 1: I AM A QUEEN

"I don't trust ants as far as I can throw them, meaning I trust them considerably more on windy days."
—Jeremy Jude

The anthill on my front lawn had been conspicuous for weeks now. I had been brainstorming how to extinguish the bothersome colony until one early morning, in the heat of the shower, I had an epiphany: I would use syrup to drown the things. Now I was standing in the yard with a towel wrapped around my waist and a bottle of syrup in my hand. The ants seemed terribly preoccupied by nothing in particular. I observed the colony for several minutes before opening the syrup's cap. I was curious to see how disruptive killing a single ant would be to the rest of the colony.

"You're very unfortunate, my friend. The odds of you being the one to perish are one in 5,424," I said to an ant drowning in a single drop of syrup. I had squeezed the syrup bottle gently, and only this ant had been caught in the drop. He rolled his tiny eyes at me as he exhaled his last breath of life. I found it curious that to humans syrup is a sweet delight, but to ants, the cause of many a massacre. Does this say something about humans? Irrelevant.

I wiped my sticky fingers on my towel as I waited for the reaction from the rest of the colony. Amazingly, there was no outrage from his fellow ants; in fact, his death seemed to have no impact whatsoever on the colony's daily routine. Only eight ants gathered around his corpse, more out of boredom than out of concern for their comrade. They gawked at his tiny body floating in the translucent drop of syrup. I couldn't help but think that if he would have been a queen ant instead of a meager worker ant, the colony would have cared much more about his death.

I've come to realize that the earth is ultimately a ball-shaped anthill filled with billions of talking ants desperate to be queens. I've been told I'm terrible with metaphors, but this one's pretty solid. Each human has, in their biology, a compulsive need to feel unique, important, and worthwhile, yet we cannot all be queen ants. Most of us are forgettable worker ants, like the dead one in the drop of syrup, or the onlookers, who had begun to get trapped in the drop because of their own greediness. Like worker ants, our ability to lift objects fifty times our weight is all we have to brag about. Queen ants, on the other hand, are crucial to the survival of the colony and could probably lift just as much as the workers if they were not pregnant all the time.

I'm sure you're wondering if I consider myself a worker ant or a queen ant; the answer is neither. I'm a human. I do, however, understand myself to be a genius, and geniuses are the queen ants of the human world; we geniuses are set apart yet essential for the survival of humanity.

I'm unsure why I decided to use an ant metaphor. I hate ants; they savagely attacked me when I was six. Hundreds of the tiny, red figures had scurried all over me and my boyish innocence. Consequently, I now held the syrup bottle over the top of the anthill, pressing and squeezing until I had poured out the entire bottle. The syrup creeped down and out over the colony like lava, drenching everything in its path. It engulfed the ants in their exact positions, and the ants' helpless, frozen bodies reminded me of the humans liquidated at Pompeii.

The point stands that life itself is fragile and uncertain for us all, is it not? Just last week, for my thirtieth birthday, I was snorkeling in Peru and nearly got chopped to pieces by a speedboat. My life flashed before my eyes, making it nearly impossible to see where I was snorkeling, but in observing my flashing life, I witnessed many memorable events and milestones. I was so awestruck by my memories that I have since decided to share them with the world through this, my life's memoir.

I'm thrilled for you, my readers! For decades— three, precisely —I've kept my inner workings and thought processes to myself due to society's misunderstandings and rash conclusions about brilliant theories; however, it is now time for me to divulge my theories. Society has been squelching the brilliance of geniuses for millennia before I even existed. For example, when Sir Isaac Newton said, "I'm going to drop these two items off of a roof," he was most certainly interrupted with a societal response such as, "Never throw things off of a roof, idiot!" If Newton had continued to be interrupted by fools, he would never have invented gravity. I've deduced that a book is the perfect medium through which to present my theories and observations in order to avoid societal interruption. By the time anyone attempts interruption, my book will already be published; thus, it will be far too late for anyone to silence me.

Before we explore in detail why I believe I'm a certified genius, I want to briefly describe the humans whose sexual intercourse resulted in my eventual existence. Merilyn is the name of my mother; She has hazel eyes and pale skin and is exactly 5'4" in stature. My father's name is Edward; he has dark brown, soulless eyes, olive skin, and a large nose. He's exactly six feet tall. Before they decided to endorse the idea of parenthood, mother was a nurse and father, a law student. When my older sister, Candice, was born, my mother quit nursing at the hospital to begin nursing her. Shortly after my sister's birth, my father passed the bar exam and moved from being an emotionless law student to an equally emotionless lawyer. Candice is six years my elder and is quite a wonderful human for a sister, but any interested readers should know she's happily married; move along.

I suppose it's only fair to mention a female I will be introducing subsequently in my life's chapters. A little foreshadow never hurts, and a little eyeshadow really makes those eyes pop (I'm only assuming; I've only worn eyeliner and blush). Her name is Lana Allen, and she's the greatest human that ever lived, but I've said too much. For now, let us begin exploration into my early years.

The human brain is said to be plastic, or malleable; in my case, it was literally the truth. I was born without a soft spot in my skull (or in my heart, according to some). The doctors were gravely concerned, as the condition is atypical of infants. I had to wear a head brace from birth to age three; my skull was shaped like that of an alien. The brace saved the symmetry and elegance of my face, but in later years, a psychiatrist told my parents the malformed skull had caused "cognitive complications." She was unaware that the malformed skull had resulted in my mind developing unprecedented levels of intelligence. Consequently, I've always found it difficult to trust the opinion of a psychiatrist.

By the age of one, I was beginning to see the world as a game of chess. I still remember the day I helped a security guard tackle a fleeing shoplifter. The guard was slow, and the thief was getting away. I was crawling down the aisle when the thief nearly stepped on my baby hand. To avoid me, he jumped and awkwardly landed on his ankle. Thus, even as an infant with limited physical capabilities, I was able to incapacitate a fully grown man. Life is a game of chess. Be the queen.

When I was two, I recall my father stopping me from sticking a metal screw into the light socket, for which I am grateful. The reason I add this as proof of brilliance is that most two-year-olds play with their toys; I explore worlds.

> *"Be not afraid if you get lost on your way to India. You may find America on accident."*
>
> *—Christopher Columbus*

According to developmental psychologists, the average three-year-old goes through a phase of asking questions about everything they see; I never went through this phase, as I already had the mind of a ten-year-old by that age. I actually didn't speak until I was five years old; I relied heavily on my observational skills.

At the tender age of four, I contracted chicken pox and pneumonia. It was a time of philosophical exploration for me; the idea of suffering fascinated me even as a four-year-old. I remember my mom telling me she'd take my pain for me if it were possible; it's still not a realistic option. There was a brief period, at age thirteen, wherein I attempted to give my pain to others via a machine I designed in my parents' garage. The design failed, as it was essentially a taser that inflicted pain on others while lacking to ease my own suffering. When it failed my dad was furious.

"You owe me a new camcorder and microwave!" he shouted. If my machine ever works, my lawyer dad will be my first subject.

The exceptional minds of our universe are the ones that take the risks no one else will. It is only because of early explorers that we now know where the end of the world lies. And, brilliant minds are not afraid to fail; I think of the great Houdini or the gentleman that invented landmines.

It is at age five that I climbed to the top of a tree. I got stuck up there for over three hours. I remember watching from above as my parents desperately searched for me. The neighbors even created a search party to help. The worst part is I was starving and desperately needing to urinate. It hadn't occurred to me to get their attention by yelling. In the end, an isolated shower got the attention of one of the neighbors.

We can all agree this was a failed exploration on my behalf, but I learned from it. Last year I got stuck in a tree again; that time, I instantly got the attention of one of the picnic attendees. Admittedly,

I forgot to yell again and was forced to resort to old habits. I noticed that humans can get away with much more when they are younger.

My dad, a corporate lawyer, bought me a bicycle for my sixth birthday. It was exactly the kind of bike a lawyer would pick out. It was expensive, painted black, and lacked training wheels. My father was lucky to have a genius son; I would not need the extra wheels.

I clearly remember, due to my photographic memory, my father pushing me to the ground from behind every time I attempted to pedal.

"I was trying to help you," he still claims to this day, but you can't trust a lawyer (pronounced "liar"). He shoved me to the ground twenty-three times until, on the twenty-fourth try, I cleverly used the violent momentum of his push to thrust me forward. My parents were amazed. Sadly, someone had cut the brakes on my bike, and I slammed into the side of my dad's BMW. He ran over to make sure I was okay, and to see if his car had scratched any paint off my bike. It had, and I was pissed—the point being, I learned to ride a bicycle on my own.

When I was seven, my parents often asked me deep, philosophical questions about right and wrong. For example, they'd ask, "Is it okay to take something from a store without paying for it?" Even as a seven-year-old, I was aware of the rarity of a parent coming to a child for advice. This hinted at something more for me; it was the first time I became aware I was not average.

I've always been favored among females; It's something I've learned to live with. My mother claims it's due to my unwavering confidence and exceptional facial features, but I know it's due to my intellectual capacity. One example of this happened when I was eight years old. On Valentine's Day, in my third grade class, our feminist teacher Miss Keller thought it was a good idea if the girls chose their Valentines. The boys just had to sit at their desks while the girls gave Valentine's Day cards to whomever they fancied. There were sixteen girls in our class, yet I somehow ended up with thirteen of the sixteen girls' cards; undoubtedly, they must have read my avant-garde-style book report on Huckleberry's Fins. People underestimate third graders' appreciation for intelligence. My mom still tries to convince me the girls thought I was cute, but she doesn't realize they thought I had contracted a disease called "cooties." Interestingly enough, it was always the most disgusted girls that seemed to have the deepest respect for my brain.

Age nine was rough. My fourth grade teacher was a militant, stern brute. She was constantly telling her students how badly they were behaving. I remember wondering who was in charge of telling her she was a miserable pessimist with no concept of the differences between children and adults. Not to mention, her teaching was so incredibly easy that an advanced brain like mine could not understand its simplicity.

Frustrated, I got myself sent to the hall. I took this opportunity to find a class better suited for me. When I entered the tenth grade class, they welcomed me as one of their own. The teacher was our neighbor and knew me well. Apparently, she had told the tenth grade girls about my brainy endeavors; they all wanted me to sit next to them to help them understand the material. Again, my mother falsely assumes the girls thought I was cute. Don't misunderstand, I am aware I am not hideous, but most humans could care less about the way a person looks.

"I just think my success as a movie star has to do with my little ol' brain and nothing else."

—Marilyn Monroe

A year later, I befriended a Mexican native by the name of Roberto. We were classmates in the fifth grade. I grew fond of Mexican culture, so much so that I developed a Mexican accent. I noticed most American names, when translated by Roberto, became

"Cabrón." They do not have too many original names in Mexico; Roberto was one of the lucky ones.

This period in my life was the first time I used my linguistic skills to learn a new language. In less than a week I was fluent in Spanish. Of course, I must have picked up on some other Spanish dialect; Roberto could not understand a word I said. Sadly, our world remains ill-prepared for the gifted minds. My teachers became deeply concerned about my new-found accent. They tattled to my parents, and thus began my adventure into the world of the insane.

CHAPTER 2: MENTAL HEALTH UNPROFESSIONALS

"No psychiatrist has ever diagnosed someone as normal."
—Jeremy Jude

There I sat in front of Dr. Baron, a certified psychiatrist specializing in close-mindedness. Before me was a wooden box with complex locks I was to open. I gave it a good try but soon realized the locks were un-unlockable.

"You seem frustrated, Jeremy," Dr. Baron said, peering at me from beneath thick, gray eyebrows. I looked up at the doctor's placid face; his calmness was almost patronizing. I deduced the purpose of the exercise was to think outside the box.

"I can do anything to solve this?" I asked.

He nodded firmly. I threw the box against the ground, splintering it into several pieces. I had solved the puzzle! Dr.Baron gasped in astonishment at my speedy problem-solving skills. He asked me many questions about my clever tactic, and soon my parents were called in to be given the good news.

I couldn't hear what Dr.Baron was telling them, but judging by their demeanor, it was overwhelmingly good news. My mother held back tears as my father consoled her. He had the same stoic face he wore every morning when he left for work and every evening when he returned home. Upon noticing me staring at them, my mother wiped her face and faked a smile; my father gave me a thumbs up and a nod. I blew a kiss at him because I enjoyed the faces he made when he was uncomfortable. My mother intercepted the kiss as my father turned away. "I love you, buddy," she mouthed. I gave her a thumbs up and a nod.

It appeared that my parents were afraid of raising a child as gifted as myself. How intimidating it must have been for them to find out that the human they birthed was far more intelligent than they were! How could they hold a normal conversation with me? How would they dispose of the useless calculators in the house? How would they spend my college fund money now that they knew I'd most likely get a full ride to Harvard? And what would this mean for my older sister, Candice? Was she now to be considered the younger sibling? These were just some of the questions swirling around in my parents' minds.

A week later I was back in Dr.Baron's office. This time he wanted me to take an I.Q. test. I glanced at my parents, who sat in the back of the room holding hands. I felt bad for them; I suppose somewhere along the line they had become my subordinates.

As soon as the doctor handed me the test, I noticed that the paper smelled faintly like vomit. I asked the doctor what brand of paper he used, but, like all close-minded individuals, he had no idea. I pulled two packets of sugar from my pocket and poured them into my mouth. They were surprisingly sweet, and I felt a new sense of motivation rush over me.

"Where did you get those?" my mother asked. The poor woman could not tell that I had obtained them from the bowl by the coffee pot in the waiting room. Everyone in the room looked at me as though I were the elephant man, and in a way, I was; elephants have extraordinary memory.

The doctor insisted we turn our attention back to the I.Q. test. He derived his entire identity from his work, and I didn't want to further lower his self-esteem, so I felt it appropriate to comply. I looked at the first question and soon realized this was not a test designed for the geniuses of our world.

This was the first question:

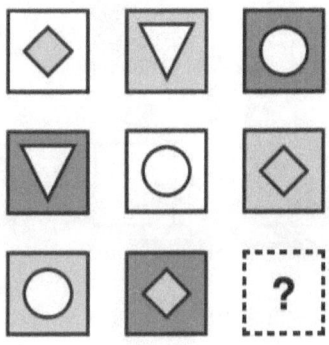

And these, the possible answers:

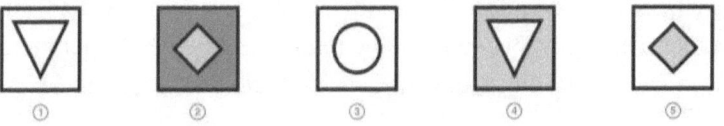

I quickly gathered that none of these answers could be correct. I glanced up at Dr.Baron and grinned; his trick question had been discovered. He was uneasy, as were my parents. I confidently grasped my pencil and did this:

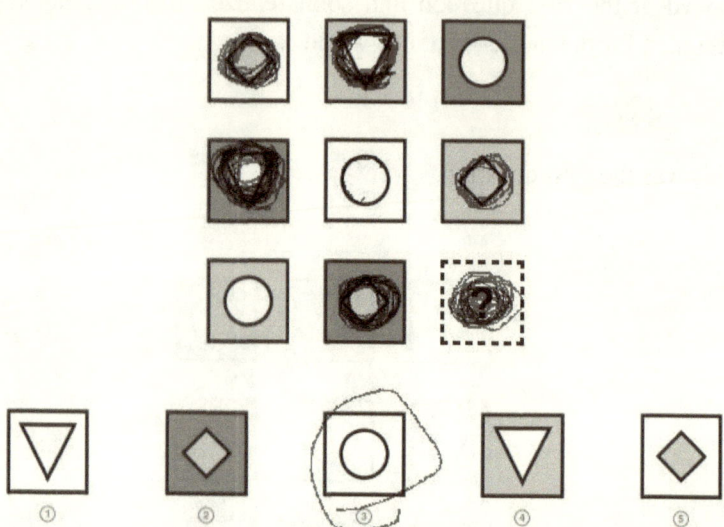

It was a simple game of "choose a shape and run with it." The doctor attempted to deceive me once more by assuring me one of the answers was correct, but I was too competent to fall for it.

I ended up with an I.Q. score of 63, but keep in mind that I was only ten, and I was a genius. Sadly, when you are gifted, standardized tests can fail to be accurate measures of your intelligence. Consider the genius Albert Einstein; he had autism. Sometimes it costs us to be in the realm of the elite. As geniuses, we often lack social skills as well as basic logic and reasoning.

My immense intelligence also explains why I was held back for a year in elementary school. The following images, created by myself, further illustrate how the mind of a genius works.

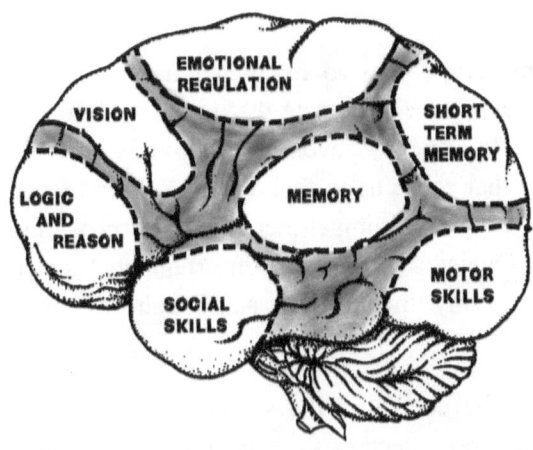

In the image above, we see the functions of the brain of an average human, such as logic and social skills. All of these average traits take up a large amount of space in the brain, leaving little room for much else. The shaded area you see is what I've defined as "academic exceptionalism"; it is what allows humans to be honor roll students. Now take a look at the brain of a genius:

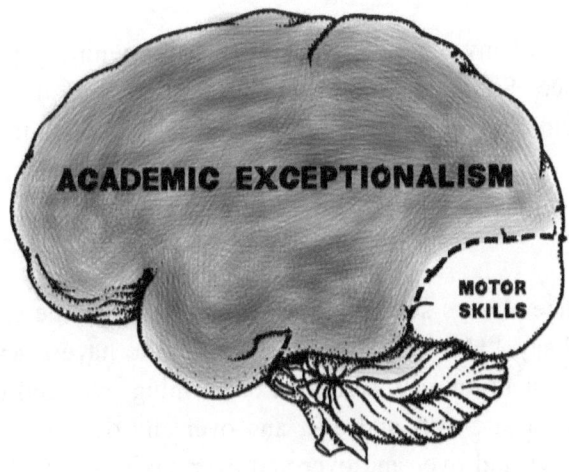

Notice that it is primarily composed of academic exceptionalism, leaving room for basic motor skills only. In some cases, geniuses don't even have room for motor skills, such as Stephen Hawking or Christopher Reeve. (Yes, Mr. Reeve's portrayal of Superman was genius.)

Considering how so many geniuses are severely behind developmentally, I feel fortunate that my parents managed to potty train me by the age of seven. We geniuses often have several impairments that cause us to feel different. I tend to think that my exceptional levels of impairment are directly linked to my exceptional levels of brilliance. Unfortunately, society seems to focus only on my impairments as though my brilliance never existed.

Over the course of the school year, my parents had me seeing behavioral specialists,therapists, and psychiatrists on a weekly basis. They put me on a medication meant to inhibit my "hyperactivity". The drugs made me feel focused, yet apathetic. My teachers were grateful for the numbing effect. Without the hindrance of my medication, I had learned to use the classroom as a platform to spread truth, but my teachers often failed to comprehend it. In their ignorance, they had often complained to my parents about my "outbursts" and "interruptions."

One of my ongoing appointments was with a psychologist named Alice. She was a timid woman with pale skin. The main thing I could not appreciate about her was that she often tried to pry into my personal life. Her interest in me was understandable. Most of her patients were lunatics and weirdos; I was a breath of fresh air to her.

Alice always started our sessions in exactly the same way. She would say, "How are you?" then ask me to have a seat. It has been said that insanity is doing the same thing over and over and over and over and over and over and over and over and over and over and over and over and over and over again. Poor Alice never became aware of her insanity.

As our sessions progressed, I found myself increasingly distracted by the ticking of the clock hanging above Alice's head. By our third session, it became too much to bear. I casually informed her that I would have to destroy her clock if it remained on the wall during our next session. She took it the wrong way. After that, all she wanted to focus on was my anger issues. I assured her repeatedly I did not have anger issues, but she didn't believe a word I said. Her lack of trust in me made me a tiny bit frustrated, so I threw her flower vase through the open window. If anything, I was doing her a favor. Flowers belong in nature. Also, her vase was hideous.

Alas, that was my last session with Alice. My parents never told me why she wouldn't see me again. I had discerned from our interactions that she was deeply depressed, so I assume she finally killed herself.

After Alice, my parents placed me in a therapy group at the local hospital. I couldn't understand why they were increasing my number of patients. After all, I could hardly help Alice with her depression, and now, at the tender age of ten, I was expected to counsel an entire group of misfits. I had the answers they needed, so how could I have refused to help? This has always been one of the struggles of being gifted: the world makes you its savior.

I stepped into the hospital on a Tuesday afternoon. I'll never forget that fresh hospital smell, the white marble floors lit by heavenly fluorescent lights, or the New York-esque hustle of nurses rushing towards a seizing grandpa. Every time I entered that lobby, I felt a sense of pride come over me. I insisted, for professionalism's sake, that my parents begin to call me doctor, but they only did so in a facetious manner. Regardless, their respect for me was not of primary importance. They were not my reason for taking the job.

I entered that first group session and was surprised to find a group of children ranging from the ages of eight to fourteen. I allowed my assistant to begin the session and listened intently for a few minutes, until I realized these children had no real mental problems. All the "issues" they described were things I did on a daily basis, such as arguing with teachers, pulling fire alarms, throwing books out windows, and other normal things humans do.

"If you'll excuse me, I must check on my other patients," I explained to my assistant as I headed to the door. She quickly stood up and practically begged me to say. I felt sorry for her; she was incompetent and deeply insecure.

"Very well, I'll stay for this session," I said.

The next week, I assured her I would be there to help, but after faking a bathroom emergency, I sneaked away to my adult patients.

As I entered the room of patients, an elderly gentleman glared at me as he shouted, "Where's the doctor? He was supposed to be here twenty-three goddamn minutes ago!"

"What an impatient patient!" I said with a chuckle. No one else got the joke.

"I apologize. It took me awhile to get away from my other patients," I said. I explained to the group that I would be leading the session. Three members felt uncomfortable with a ten-year-old therapist. After accusing me of being an impostor, they decided to leave. That left the group with three patients with schizophrenia, two with highly functioning autism, one addicted to black tar heroin, and one with a brilliant mind full of profound advice. (That last one was me.)

The first person I counseled was an elderly schizophrenic by the name of David. He tearfully expressed the pain of having to quit his job because of all the distractions going on in his head. His wife had also recently left him.

"David, what's the real problem here?" I asked.

"I'm lonely," he explained.

"No, you're not. Think of all the little friends in your head you've talked to today. You're never truly alone." David decided to leave the session at that point. My words had given him the resolution he'd been searching for.

Margie, a single mother with no children and strong heroin tendencies, spoke up next. She expressed to the group that she felt out of control and she did not know how to cope. She confessed that heroin made her feel such ecstasy, but that afterwards she would have suicidal thoughts. As a ten-year-old, I could comprehend Margie's situation in its entirety.

"Margie, when I was six, I became addicted to chocolate milk, so much so that I nearly gave up on all other drinks. You know what I did? I started mixing small amounts of chocolate milk with other drinks so I always had what I wanted. And no, I didn't enjoy my orange juice with chocolate milk, but guess what? I eventually made it through the pain and learned to drink things again without the chocolate milk."

My advice to her was the same—to use just enough heroin to not feel suicidal. She loved the idea. I also advised her to try chocolate milk since it was, in my opinion, better than heroin. She loved that idea a little less.

My session was interrupted by another doctor, who would eventually become my friend and co-therapist, Dr. Aust. He entered the room and promptly took over the class.

"Who are you?" he asked.

"I could ask you the same thing, Doctor," I replied as I offered him my hand. He escorted me back to the children's group where he asked me to keep an eye on the children. I knew the doctor was trying to take over my other group, but I wasn't worried; we both knew I was the better therapist.

Over the course of several weeks, I showed up to my adult group only to find Dr. Aust attempting to counsel the group without me. "Damn it, Doctor! This is a team effort!" I'd say, at which point he'd pathetically ask my permission to counsel the group just that once. This went on for weeks. I'd show up to my sessions early to give advice to the needy, and he'd again plead with me to teach the children's group instead. Needless to say, our partnership began to deteriorate. There were times I felt Dr. Aust treated me like one of his patients. This tension between us was bad for my group, so I decided to relinquish my position as co-therapist.

The week after my resignation, Dr. Aust asked me to visit with him in his office regarding an important matter. I was initially suspicious about his intent since we had become nemeses; he and I were like Moriarty and Sherlock. I entered the room and sat at his desk without saying a word.

"Jeremy Jude, thank you for coming!" he said as he shook my hand.

"What's this about, Doctor?" I asked.

"Your parents tell me you have very little patience with people," he said. I was about to punch him in the throat until he added, "In our line of work, Jeremy, there are a lot of idiots."

It was the first thing he'd said to me that made any sense, and I could feel a bond forming between us. He scratched his scruffy face; I scratched my eyeball on accident. He continued, "The reason I brought you here is to ask for your help as a fellow doctor."

"I'm listening," I said, although I was just returning from a daydream.

"These stupid people, that make you and me angry...sometimes they want to hear what we have to say, but they don't know how to handle our intelligence. For example, one time I was mad at a friend for not removing his shoes when he entered my house, so I threw a vase at him."

I nearly leapt to my feet, excited to find someone so like minded. "Doctor, I did that exact thing to a psychologist named Alice!"

He smiled. "The problem I face, Jeremy, is that throwing the vase did not help my friend take off his shoes, because he did not understand my logic of throwing the vase at him."

"Precisely, Doctor. It goes over their heads."

"Yes. But, I'd like you to visit me once a week to help me figure out how I could have gotten that idiot to take off his shoes in a way that he understood."

"Why would you want that?"

"Don't you want people to listen to you?"

"It honestly depends on the person."

In the end, I agreed to help Moriarty—though now my Watson—to learn how to deal with average plebeians. My parents were thrilled to have me instruct Dr. Aust on a weekly basis. They finally understood what I was capable of and eventually allowed me to leave therapy altogether.

My brilliance would remain unseen for the next few years. I attempted to branch off and counsel thirteen other groups, but I found each of my co-therapists to be just as abrasive as Dr. Aust had originally been. The world was not ready for a ten-year-old psychiatrist (except Dr. Aust). I gave him advice until I turned fourteen. We stopped when he told me he'd learned the basics of communicating with people in a way they'd understand. Things were finally turning around for him.

With my career as a mental health professional behind me, I would soon progress to another level of savantism through music.

CHAPTER 3: MUSICOLOGY

Winter was upon us. My eighth grade class and I were on our way to Chicago to visit the science museum. Snow poured down around the busy highway. Mr. Newman, our bus driver, was driving at half speed, hunched over the steering wheel and squinting at the road through the giant snowflakes. He had declined my initial offer to drive the bus for him, and now he was suffering the consequences.

Our teacher Miss Carter announced to the class that we would not make it in time for our appointment at the museum. She explained that she had even tried to call the museum to reschedule, but to no avail. I was okay with not going to the museum. With cognition like mine, it is difficult to be impressed by science. She announced that the alternate plan would be to have hot chocolate and donuts at a local donut shop called Dunkin' Donuts. The class cheered, but I was too busy counting the skyscrapers to applaud. (There were twenty-seven.)

Upon entering Dunkin' Donuts, we were hit with the sweet smell of vanilla and fried dough. We were also hit with an eyefull of locals. Never in my life had I experienced such culture shock. There was enough diversity in that shop to fill the entire color spectrum. Seeing my classmates' happy faces as they devoured their donuts annoyed me terribly; it was time for a stroll.

I stepped out into the cold with the intent to walk towards the tallest skyscraper I could see. More learning took place for me that day than the rest of the school year. My first lesson was on the invisibility of black ice; I still have the scar on my left elbow. I met a lot of ingenious people like myself on the streets. They had some amazing theories about our world. Unfortunately, our conversations often ended short when they'd ask me for a dollar and I'd tell them I had no money. Perhaps it was for the best. These particular geniuses smelled like they did not utilize the common practice of bathing and exhibited a poor sense of fashion.

As I continued my journey, I saw many other geniuses like those, but I no longer stopped to talk with them. Some of them were so brilliant they seemed to lack all common sense. One of the geniuses barked at me like a dog. I thought about this interaction for days but could never find the meaning behind it. I was truly in the presence of greatness.

I finally made it downtown, where the skyscrapers surrounded me. I passed by an outdated Macy's building. I discovered more black ice on the ground; I still have the scar on my right knee. At the end of the next block, a crowd of humans had gathered around another street genius as he angrily hit on plastic buckets with a pair of drumsticks. The crowd seemed to feel pity for him; some people even tossed money into the hat he had dropped on the ground. He was in for quite a treat the next time he put on his hat!

As I listened to the man play, I heard something this crowd would never hear. My mind turned this genius's beat—a seemingly mindless rage to the rest of society—into a rhythmic pattern. The sound I was hearing was the heartbeat of Africa—or possibly Canada. (I have yet to memorize the heartbeats of continents.) My eyes were opened to the world of music, and my hands would soon follow.

This moment of deep revelation was ruined by a police officer asking if I was with Elmore Middle School. It was really none of his business, so I told him to get into his car and go. That's exactly what he did, but he decided to put me into the car as well. I began to fear I had been kidnapped, until I saw Dunkin' Donuts ahead, where a furious Miss Carter stood in the parking lot.

I slowly exited the car police car. The class was already on the bus. I stared into my teacher's fiery blue eyes and said, "Miss Carter, if I were a modern Beethoven, would you still be mad?"

She insisted she would be. I doubt Miss Carter had any idea who was standing before her; at the time, even *I* had no idea that I was standing before myself as a genius.

I returned home that day with a pair of drumsticks I had commandeered from the bandroom. My parents greeted me with a warm frown of disappointment. They blamed themselves as parents for the incident in Chicago. They thought my behavior was because they had forgotten to refill my prescriptions, but they didn't know I had been dumping my prescription pills in the toilet for weeks before the prescription had run out. They also didn't understand that the true reason for my wandering in the big city was my obsession with exploration and discovery. I learned more in the city than I did at Dunkin' Donuts, and much more than I ever would have learned at a science museum. Still, when I tried to explain my cognitive processes to them, they could not fully understand them, so I let them think what they wanted. I had more important things that required my attention.

In the experimental phase of drumming, I first needed to find the right materials on which to practice. The majority of my tests consisted of using kitchen supplies to find the perfect sounds. It took me ten days to find adequate surfaces. Below is a list of drum-worthy versus non-drum-worthy equipment. Note that all materials were tested for objectivity.

DRUM-WORTHY	NON-DRUM-WORTHY
Metal pots	Glass bowls
Plastic buckets	China plates
Tupperware	Human heads
Plastic jars	Windows
Drums	Pudding
Tabletops	Computer screens

I spent days intensely practicing on my drumming equipment until my father confiscated my drumsticks. He claimed he had stacks of paperwork he needed to finish and was unable to focus because of my constant noise-making, but I knew he was lying; he was a lawyer. Furthermore, his growing jealousy of my talent was too strong to keep hidden. My mother, in an attempt to diffuse the escalating conflict between my father and me, suggested I join the marching band at school. I laughed in her face. She thought I was scoffing, but in reality, I was laughing out of the pure joy of hearing the only good idea my mother had ever had.

The first day of band practice was not what I had expected. I was surrounded by strange-looking people. Travis, our talentless tuba player, was as large as a tuba would be if it were human; thus, I referred to his tuba as "the twin." Next to him was Caleb, the faulty flute player. Only he could manage to be out of breath before we even began playing. He claimed it was asthma, but I knew it was really because he was out of shape— literally. His spine had a peculiar "s" curve to it. To my left was Kimberly. She seemed to think talking was an instrument, as each time the band began to play she was still finishing a sentence. I wasn't attracted to Kimberly's personality in the slightest, but we did have an odd sexual tension between us. She also played a mean snare drum, so I decided to let her into our drum section despite her incessant chattering.

Our band teacher, Mr. B, eagerly addressed the class as his "little prodigies." I scoffed loudly enough for him to hear me through his unruly, unnecessarily curly hair. I knew he meant it in a charmingly casual manner, but it was insulting for him to call other members of the class prodigies when I, an actual prodigy, was present. I suppose I was expecting too much from Mr. B though. It was he who had once waxed his legs before substitute teaching gym class. He had forced the gym class to play leapfrog, which was less than enjoyable from the start, but it became unbearably uncomfortable when he joined in on the fun. It's a strange thing to see a grown man jump over you in revealing shorts. I reminded the professor it was "leap frog," not "leap testicles." It was not an especially clever thing for a genius to say, but I was fourteen, and it got the point across.

Mr. B passed around the sheet music, which I unaffectionately referred to as shit music. (People do not understand how rigid and unromantic sheet music is.) Loudmouth Kimberly attempted to tell on me for saying "shit." I told her I did not say "shit," to which she replied, "But you said it just then." It would have been a tragedy to be removed from my position as head snare leader over such a trifling matter. I did the only rational thing a man can do to get a woman to stop talking: I leaned in and kissed her. To my delight, she gazed at me without uttering another word. She didn't tell on me about the shit music, but Mr. B witnessed my romantic gesture and sent me to the principal's office for kissing a girl.

On my way out, I noticed Travis guffawing at me. He laughed like Santa Claus, if Santa were twenty pounds heavier and hated himself. I shared this thought out loud with the whole class. I never heard Travis laugh again. Actually, he transferred to a new school the next day. I hope he had a jollier time at his new school.

I sat in front of Mr. Kavitzch, the stern school principal with a hidden soft heart. He asked me why I had been sent to him. I explained that I wanted Kimberly removed from my drum circle and that Mr. B should "B" let go.

Mr. Kavitzch didn't laugh at my pun. He kept an excellent poker face, but I knew he secretly wanted to help me. I offered him front seats at the next marching band concert (an offer I could not actually make happen). The principal called my bluff and asked again why I had been sent to his office. I began to explain to him that Kimberly and I were deeply in love and could not keep our hands off each other, but he interrupted, shifting uncomfortably in his seat and telling me that was "enough" information. Kimberly and I were not in love, but I have found that most adults get squirmy when a teenager speaks to them regarding sexual issues. They fear listening because they do not want to appear to have pedophelic levels of interest. I used this discomfort to my advantage throughout my adolescence. I've never used this tactic on priests, though, as I have heard it has no effect on them.

After warning me not to get handsy in class, Mr. Kavitzch sent me back to band practice. I re-entered the band room, from which came the horrific sounds of my peers' best musical efforts and Kimberly's shrill voice. Mr. B looked up at me in shock and slight disgust, as he had not expected me to return. I explained to him that his superior had sent me back to class with a slap on the wrist and a pat on the back.

"We'll see about that!" Mr. B exclaimed, marching out of the room with his chin pointed upward and his nostrils flared. If only he had known that Mr. Kavitzch was my ally!

I saw Mr. B's absence as my opportunity to finally teach the class true music. My first order of business was to kick Caleb out of the class. I knew he would not put up a fight since a blow to his chest would likely kill him. The rest of the students initially protested my decision, but they were ultimately too lazy and adolescent to pose any real challenge to my authority.

Caleb scurried out of the room without looking at me. As he

exited, I glanced at Kimberly, still chatting away. I decided to keep her around since Mr. Kavitzch thought we were a couple.

"Moving on, class," I said. "Please pass up your shit music."

They all stared at me blankly.

"Class, pass up the shit music or you're all suspended," I declared. I hated being the bad guy, but they needed a stronger leader than Mr. B. My main disappointment in this moment was Kimberly's lack of loyalty to me. Even after all we had been through as a fake couple, she now scoffed at me defiantly. She cackled with betrayal, and I was certain we were over. While Kimberly hadn't caused me any real pain, I was concerned that Mr. Kavitzch would be devastated at the news of our breakup.

I turned my attention back to the class. A handful of students had reluctantly passed up their shit music, and my next step of action was to find out if I had any competition in the band. I asked my students if any of them had any form of musical giftedness. From the back of the class a future dropout shouted, "Why don't you sit down, dude?" to which I replied, "Because I'm better than you." The insolence of the scraggly-haired teen was astounding. I was considering whether to throw a nearby chalkboard eraser at the kid when Martha, a classic snobby mathlete, told me she had "perfect pitch."

I laughed in her face and told her pitch had nothing to do with music. "If you have a perfect pitch," I explained, "then I suggest you join the softball team. After all, you already have the masculine build of a softball player." Telling a girl she has the build of a softball player, I have since discovered, is more often taken as an insult than a compliment.

"I'm telling the principal!" she exclaimed. She headed to Mr. Kavitzch's office to tell him of her newfound softball pursuit. She seemed oddly furious about quitting the band, but I deduced it was due to the usual mixed feelings a human experiences when in transition.

I asked once more if there were any musically gifted students in my class, but no one responded. After a few strongly worded coercions, I managed to get a student named Adam to raise his hand. He was quiet and kept to himself most of the time. I loathe to admit it, but he was well versed at playing the saxophone. He looked at me with wide eyes and said, "I have synesthesia."

I ordered him to go directly to the nurse's office without touching anything. He remained in his seat, though, and explained that synesthesia is when a person experiences musical notes as colors. For example, an "E" chord would be blue and a "D" chord would be yellow. He told the class it was easy for him to learn a song because he could see the music with his eyes. Society calls people like him "savants" or "brilliant" or "prodigies", but I call them cheaters. Everything is easier when it is color coded. I reminded Adam that music is about hearing, not seeing. I told him to join art class instead, but he ignored me. I made a mental note to inform Mr. Kavitzch of Adam's lack of academic integrity.

With any chance of competition ruled out, I began my lecture. "Before we begin, let us take a moment of silence for the slaughter of innocent notes that has taken place in this room," I said, lowering my head in reverence.

The moment of silence was interrupted by a furious Mr. B and an authoritative (but secretly supportive) Mr. Kavitzch. Trailing behind them were Martha—especially unattractive in her current state of defiance—and Caleb with his eyes still moist from tears.

"I'm in the middle of my lecture, gentlemen," I said sternly. Over-reacting to the situation, Mr. B commanded me to accompany him and Mr. Kavitzch to the office. On my way out, I winked at Mr. Kavitzch; we had each other's backs. He dissimulated his friendship with me by warning me not to wink at him again. I would not have expected anything less from this admirable soul. I felt bad for Mr. B. He had no idea he was about to be metaphorically gang banged by us, much like a sheep led to its slaughter. I blew Kimberly a final air kiss for appearances' sake, which she strangely caught with her middle finger.

In the principal's office, I quickly realized that Mr. Kavitzch would be unable to break his cover for fear of losing his job. It occurred to me that if he replaced Mr. B with a fourteen-year-old genius, he would have surely been condemned by society. Additionally, Mr. B was Jewish and a closeted gay man. If Mr. Kavitzch tried to fire him, Mr. B could have easily sued for homosemetism. ("Homosemetism" is one of many words I have coined. It means "Hatred for or discrimination against homosexual Jews." I've also coined the terms "whoretelectual," "angreep," and "fatthlete.")

I knew it was time for me to resign as the band instructor. In fact, it was time for me to move on altogether. This school had no room for a human like me. I nodded at Mr. Kavitzch as if to say, "It has been a pleasure working with you." I then proceeded to strategically swing my arm into Mr. B's cup of coffee, which had been sitting precariously on the desk in front of him. The act was excessive, granted, but in my defense, I had thought the coffee was lukewarm. I held back a smile as I watched Mr. B jump out of his seat with a quick scream, wiping frantically at his now coffee-stained pants. I knew Mr. Kavitzch was having a good laugh on the inside, which always warmed my heart.

I was expelled within the hour.

Later that night, my mom wept in my father's arms. "I just don't know what to do with him any more," she said.

My lawyer dad patted her gingerly on the head and replied, "We could put him back on medication."

"But he's miserable when he takes it!"

"The psychiatrist can adjust his dose."

"Edward, honey, I don't want him on medication any more. He's not happy on it."

"Merilyn, he poured coffee on a teacher. The teacher had third-degree burns. That's what we're dealing with!"

My mom began to quietly sob into my father's cold shoulder again.

I was able to hear their entire conversation in detail since I was hiding in the coat closet nearby. Around that time in my life, I had been exploring the idea of espionage. I practiced hiding in many places, until one fateful night when I hid under my parents' bed. After some boring conversation I couldn't understand, the passions of youth overcame my parents unexpectedly. It was perhaps the worst thing that has ever happened to me.

From the coat closet, I shook my head. My reasons for resigning from that school would be incomprehensible to my parents. I felt how Jesus—an astute man with disloyal friends—must have felt when he ran away from his parents to teach the elders of the temple how to play the horn. I could see that my musical brilliance was causing people around me to suffer, first with Mr. Kavitzch's career, then Mr. B's third-degree burn, and now with my parents' emotional instability. Just as Jesus gave up the horn to become a simple carpenter, I decided to give up my life of music to save the world around me. And sure enough, three days later I rose from my bed with a new objective: driving.

CHAPTER 4: DRIVER'S ED

"Bumping into an old friend is unpleasant when you're both still inside your vehicles."
-Jeremy Jude

I ran into the kitchen where my parents and my sister were eating breakfast. (My sister was visiting home from college for the holidays.) I told my parents it was time for me to get my driver's license. They attempted to squelch my idea by reminding me I could not legally get a learner's permit until I turned fifteen. My sister said it was too bad I didn't live in Michigan, because a person only had to be fourteen to get a permit in that state.

Since I had the mental age of two full-grown adults I decided to teach myself how to drive. I located my dad's car keys and GPS and began my first lesson. I quickly learned that "D" meant "forward," which made no logical sense. That first lesson cost my dad one headlight and a mountain bike. Next, I learned that "R" meant "backwards" which, again, made no sense.

I programmed the car's GPS navigation device to take me to a Department of Motor Vehicles branch in Michigan. Driving was tricky at first, even for someone with a learning ability like mine. The driving got easier once I made it onto the highway, where there were no more traffic signals making extraneous suggestions. The

GPS calculated that I was seven hours and thirty-two minutes away from getting my permit. That would be plenty of time to familiarize myself with the car.

As I drove, I experimented with various functions of the car, but found them relatively unhelpful. One particularly pointless function was a button with a red triangle. It was meant to be used as a turn signal for the indecisive or the dyslexic; I was neither of those. I did discover one useful function—the autopilot button. Unfortunately, it malfunctioned for me and I had to jump back into the driver's seat before the car veered completely off the road. At least it kept the car going at a steady speed.

One hour into the trip, police lights went off behind me. They were quite distracting, but I did my best to keep my eyes on the road ahead. Five minutes later, five more police cars with lights flashing appeared behind me. I waved at them to pass me up, but they did not understand the gesture. I felt like a mother goose trying to get her baby geese to stop following her. After a minute of this, it occurred to me that the officers were lost and that they had seen my GPS through my car window. They were expecting me to lead them. This was yet another time in my life where my brilliance was needed. Here I was, a fourteen-year-old genius, my first time driving, being endowed as the chief of police by a group of squad cars from Michigan.

Thinking they needed directions, I pulled to the side of the road and slowed to a stop. I had planned to walk over to them, but two officers had jumped out their cars and walked so briskly to my car that they were at my door before I even opened it.

I was met with stares that made it clear that my reign as chief was not going to last. I felt betrayed, not only by my parents, who had told the police that I had stolen my dad's car, but also by the police, who had turned on me.

I was placed in the back of a police car as if I were some sort of lawbreaker instead of their comrade. I leaned in to Officer Hugel's ear and whispered, "You're better than this." His tough guy facade almost broke, and for a millisecond, I swear I saw his eyes well with tears. I wasn't angry with him; he was possibly a rookie who simply lacked experience. I decided it best not to lower his self-esteem any further.

The ride home was grueling. Officer Hugel's partner, Officer Moody, asked me several unusual questions, including, "Do you think it'd be fun to live behind bars?"

I told Officer Moody I did not know but that I could find out for him. You would think that of all people, a police officer would know the answer to this question. At one point he told me, "Son, this road you're going down won't end well." I assured him the road was fine as I had traveled on it only minutes ago.

I asked Officer Hugel if we could stop at an Olive Garden to celebrate us reaching the halfway mark back to my hometown. When he refused, I lied and told him they sold donuts. I had heard this strategy would work on a police officer, but he chose a Wendy's drive-through instead. He ordered three hamburgers, two coffees, and a water. The water was for me. I requested they order me a coffee as well, but Officer Moody said coffee was the last thing I needed. It crossed my mind to explain the health benefits coffee would have on me, such as antioxidants, but he was a police officer. I was unsure about whether he knew what an antioxidant was, and I certainly did not want to embarrass him in front of Officer Hugel. The last thing any officer of the law needs is to be humiliated by a brilliant fourteen-year-old.

For the remainder of the trip, I pretended to be a dumb, average boy. I even peed myself a tiny bit to create the full effect. It worked. By the time I got home, the officers felt they were better than me. As their ex-chief of police, nothing could have made me feel prouder than to see their renewed self-confidence at that moment. The officers walked me to the door, at which point I turned to salute them. "I'm so proud of you both," I said sincerely.

My mom opened the door and tearfully embraced me. "We were so worried!" she exclaimed.

Officers Hugel and Moody took this opportunity to leave without saying goodbye. No goodbyes were necessary between us; that was the kind of relationship I had developed with my officers.

My mom walked me to the kitchen, where my dad sat with murderous eyes next to my sister, Candice. My mom and sister both stared at me with unnecessary concern. My mom reminded my dad to speak calmly.

"Why would you do something like this?" he asked in a repressed tone.

"Sometimes, when you're the chief of police, you have to make unpopular decisions," I replied. I could see his jaw tighten and relax again in silence. His murderous look was fervent, but I knew it was just his jealousy popping up again. He looked at my mom and shook his head.

My mom placed her hand on his wrist and said, "It's okay, honey. why don't you leave the room for a bit?" He took her advice.

My sister asked me if I truly thought I was the chief of police.

"No...not any more," I replied.

My mom then asked if at some point in time I thought I had been the chief of police. This line of questioning got old for me. It was the same line of questioning they had used before when I was a psychiatrist, the CEO of a hotel, a film director, and a band teacher at my school. It was difficult for them to believe that a fourteen-year-old could hold such prestigious positions. In their ignorance, they could not recognize that I was not an average boy. Even I had not fully realized I was a genius yet. I knew I was brilliant and gifted, but it would be a while before I was certain I was a genius, and even longer before I felt comfortable calling myself a genius in front of other humans.

My dad returned to the kitchen and sat down rigidly in a chair across the room from us.

"Are you okay, Ed?" asked my mom.

He nodded. "I've thought about it," he began, "and I don't think we'll let you take driver's ed next year."

I was glad we were on the same page. "No need!" I said. "I learned everything I need to know on the road to Michigan."

My sister looked at my parents with renewed concern. "Mom, have you had him looked at for psychosis?" she asked ignorantly. She was a chemistry major at the time and knew nothing about the human brain.

"What is that?" My mom asked, indulging my sister's pitiful theorizing.

"It's like head lice, but on the lower region of the body," I explained.

"No, it's not," said my sister. She naively explained how some people with symptoms of psychosis think they are the greatest at everything and suffer from delusions of grandeur. I assured my parents she was wrong and reminded them that my opinion as a retired psychiatrist far outweighed her uneducated guess. My protests were in vain, though. They listened to her simply because she was older and in college.

I agreed to be tested for psychosis on the condition that when I turned fifteen, they would allow me to get my permit. I had learned the value of compromise by then: giving someone what they wanted was somewhat satisfying when I was also able to benefit from the arrangement. This is called a "win/win" situation, but I'm also satisfied with a "win/lose" situation, depending on the winner. We had a deal, and I was ready to play along with their game.

The plan unfortunately backfired, as the psychiatrist we saw incorrectly designated my brilliance as psychosis and gave me an absurd batch of diagnoses along with it: psychotic disorder not otherwise specified, intermittent explosive disorder, and early signs of antisocial personality disorder.

I felt bad for my parents. They took all mental health professionals' words as truth. Of course, I had learned long ago not to trust their labels. I had been diagnosed with six different illnesses by said professionals by the time I was twelve, which led me to deduce that none of these could be correct. None of the diagnoses fully explained my "symptoms," as they called them, nor did it seem efficient to have six different diagnoses fitting only some of my characteristics. It wasn't until later that I realized that what society had labeled as an illness was really me being a genius. It was the simplest and most logical explanation for the misunderstood life I had lived.

Now my parents believed I had psychosis, among other things, which caused them unnecessary amounts of stress and suffering. I had to move on from the unfortunate event and focus on my part of the deal. Soon I would be fifteen, and I was ready to drive.

A few months later, my parents signed me up for driver's education. Taking the class was more of a legal formality since I'd already learned how to drive. The school was located between a laundromat and a hot dog restaurant; it became clear to me that completing my driving hours in a Ferrari as I had wanted to do was now extremely unlikely.

The room held roughly thirty students and one mediocre, balding professor with thick bottle-cap glasses; I named him Greggors. He was about eighty years old and ill- equipped to teach these students. His trembling hands and bent knees led me to believe he had been in several car accidents over the course of his life. I deduced that this poor man was only teaching the class because he had lost his retirement savings in a pyramid scheme. Whatever the case, he needed my help.

I listened attentively as Greggors made a fool of himself. I was waiting for the right moment to jump in and save him. While listening, I kept noticing a pair of beautiful green eyes next to me glancing in my direction every few seconds. The eyes belonged to a girl with the most adorable features I had ever seen. Her wavy dark hair, her pale skin, her perfectly thin nose, her freckles, and her elegant, aristocratic neck formed a figure whose beauty was second only to Nefertiti herself. Still, her staring was distracting. Greggors was drowning in his own ocean of despair, and I missed my cue to jump in and rescue the man.

"Why are you staring at me?" I asked the adorable girl.

She was flustered and didn't know what to say. She moved her gaze back to her book and pretended to read. Eventually I found myself staring at her, too. She was no longer giving me looks, which strangely lured me. I had completely neglected Greggy boy at this point. The mind of a genius is odd in that in one moment you're trying to solve $E=mc^2$, but in the next moment, a far more complex problem comes along that makes you forget $E=mc^2$ ever existed. It's another trial we geniuses must bear.

No human had ever controlled my heart rate; that is, until I met this girl. I sat with sweating palms, accelerated heart rate, dry mouth, and a form of paralysis unknown to me, unable to keep myself from glancing in her direction. For years, I had assumed shyness resulted from brain damage, but now I, an individual with a perfectly healthy brain, found myself unable to speak. This girl seemed to control my physiological states. When she glanced up at the board to take notes, I felt it in my stomach. At one point I caught her glancing up at me; this caused severe damage to my cardiovascular health because I felt my heart loosen and drop two inches into my chest cavity. There was a supernatural element to our interactions. No words were spoken, yet it was the most interesting conversation I'd ever had.

I fought my body and won back the courage to speak. I leaned over to her and whispered, "I am Jeremy."

She looked at me with an odd half-smile. Her cheeks turned red, and I wondered if I was also having some sort of effect on her.

"I'm Lana," she whispered back as she fidgeted with the gold necklace around her neck. I deduced the necklace was a source of comfort for her as she seemed to touch it when she was nervous.

"Lana, is your heart beating faster than normal as well?" I asked. She didn't answer, but her cheeks substantially increased in redness. She drew her eyes down as though she were afraid to look at me again. I must have amused her, though, because she grinned widely.

At the end of class, I looked into her eyes and said, "Lana, while I respect you, I cannot allow you to manipulate my body. This hold you have over my mind and heart is too much. We should sit separately from now on." She was confused and devastated, which surprised me, considering there were seventeen other boys for her to pursue in class. I too was devastated. The thought of her with another man made me feel strange. I secretly wanted her to have a hold on me, even if it was damaging to my cardiovascular health.

A few days later, I sat on the stairs of my porch waiting for the driving instructor to pick me up. It was cold. My mother insisted I wait inside, but I refused. She brought me a coat and advised me to always listen to my instructor.

"Always?" I asked, raising an eyebrow at her. My mom nodded firmly. "What if she tells me to crash into a grocery store? Shall I?" I asked.

People often fail to consider the possible consequences of blindly obeying orders. The German people never said no to Hitler, and it did not end well. I am not saying my mother is comparable to Hitler, but I do believe the similarity in their love for obedience creates enough suspicion to at least question my mother's motives.

My mother kissed me on the cheek and went inside. A few minutes later, my dad emerged from the house in a hurry, running late to a deposition. "Bye, I'm late! I'll be back at seven!" he blurted as he shut the door to his BMW. He resembled the rabbit from Alice In Wonderland.

As my father peeled off, a terribly green car pulled up to my driveway. I hold nothing against green, but it is such an unpleasant color on cars, especially when the shade of green resembles the color of vomit. I read somewhere that geniuses hate green, and I don't think that is mere coincidence.

I peered into the driver's side window and was startled to find Lana Allen in the driver's seat. She rolled down the window as the instructor in the passenger seat, Miss Patty, explained that Lana and I would be taking turns driving. I recognized that my chances of dying in a car crash because of a novice driver like Lana were high, but I didn't mind the risk.

"Is that Lana Allen?" Shouted my mother from the porch. She walked over to the drivers side to greet her.

"Hi Mrs. Jude," said Lana.

"Have you met my son, Jeremy?"

"Yeah, we met in class."

"Good! Well, tell your parents I say hi, okay?"

"I will."

Little did I know, my parents had been close friends with Lana's parents for years. When I was fourteen, I went with my mom to a baby shower they'd hosted at their house; Lana wasn't there since she traveled most weekends for debate team or tennis matches. We had never met since we went to different schools, and I had no interest in visiting the Allens with my parents. I assumed their daughter was a different Lana Allen than the one I met in driving school. I also somehow assumed the Allens died in a plane crash some time ago; I'm still unsure why. I got into the back seat, and Lana backed out of the driveway and followed Miss Patty's driving instructions.

I watched Lana's eyes through the rear view mirror as she drove. A strange paradox was unfolding inside me: On the one hand, I wanted Lana to stare back at me, but on the other hand, I needed her to keep her eyes on the road. In situations like these, I wished she were cockeyed; in any other situation her front-facing eyes would have done just fine.

I was devolving into a stupid person. Whenever Lana was in my presence, all my brilliance seemed to evaporate. Thirty minutes had passed, and all I had learned was that the freckles on Lana's cheeks brought out the cuteness of her nose. At Miss Patty's prompting, Lana pulled into a parking lot so that she and I could switch places. I leaned over to Miss Patty and said, "Miss Patty, I need you to sit in the back so Lana can sit next to me."

She laughed as though I were joking. I had not noticed the extra steering wheel in the passenger seat until that moment. Never before had I seen a car designed for England and America all at once. "Miss Patty, don't attempt to drive while I'm the driver seat, please," I implored. Both of us driving at once would have certainly caused some sort of malfunction.

Again, she laughed as though I were joking. Lana cracked a smile, too. I enjoyed seeing Lana smile, so I allowed this moment to pass without conflict.

"Asshole!" yelled Miss Patty as a driver in a pickup truck flew past us through a school zone. She blushed as she turned to me and sheepishly said, "Pardon my French."

As a savant, I am a master of many languages, French being one of them, and what Miss Patty had said was not French. Perhaps it made her feel more cultured. Driving instructors have a hard life, so I decided against correcting her. I decided to pursue the asshole in the truck to pull him over; you can take the man away from the police force, but you can't take the police away from the manforce. I stepped on the accelerator and aimed my sights ahead.

"What are you doing!?" yelled Miss Patty. "Stop!" She stepped on the brakes from her side of the car, and I watched as the criminal drove out of sight. I was furious, but I felt pity for Miss Patty. She'd embarrassed herself in front of Lana and me.

For the rest of the hour I drove without saying a word, and without making a mistake. Occasionally I would glance through the rear view mirror at Lana. She would smile at me, at which point Miss Patty would warn me I was veering into oncoming traffic. It was in these moments that I wished *I* was cock-eyed.

I didn't feel like entertaining Miss Patty's chiding; I was in a rather dark mood. Her stopping me from chasing the truck reminded me of how so many ambitions I'd had in my life had been suffocated by society over and over again. Everyone wants to be a genius, but no one truly understands how troubled a genius must often be. We are "freaks" and "heroes" simultaneously, all the while being hopelessly misunderstood.

The genius artist, Salvador Dali, melted a bunch of clocks on tree branches. Society called it art, but as a fellow genius I assure you he did so to stop the ticking noises; geniuses hate the sound of a ticking clock.

We geniuses also ignore people when we feel acknowledging them wastes time. The genius composer, Ludwig Van Beethoven, is said to have gone deaf for the last decade of his life; I assure you he was not deaf, but rather chose to ignore other humans so he could focus on his work. Professor Helen Keller used a similar approach when she was tired of answering her student's vacuous questions.

Now, I again felt that I was being placed into a category, this time by Miss Patty; I worried that Lana would begin to think the same of me.

"You missed your turn, dear," said Miss Patty.

I was too busy smiling at Lana to notice the turn. Miss Patty told me to pull into the next gas station to turn around. She was beginning to "chap my ass," as the expression goes. Her desire to control this casual date between Lana and myself needed to be put to a stop. I decided to redirect us using my own methods. Without giving notice, I turned the wheel sharply and slammed on the brakes. My maneuver would have been seamless had Miss Patty's pudgy, uncoordinated hands not grabbed the second steering wheel. This lack of judgment on her part caused the vehicle to slam into a street light on the other side of the road.

Cars behind us honked at Miss Patty for ruining the perfect drift. Miss Patty and Lana were frazzled and disoriented. I was a little overwhelmed by the situation myself, but I managed to remember that cars were very likely to explode after crashes. I had to save Lana; I could address my disappointment in Miss Patty later. I hastily unbuckled my seatbelt, jumped out of the car, and threw open Lana's backseat door. By now, Lana had somehow managed to unbuckle her own seatbelt. I pulled her out of the car and carried her in my arms to safety. I didn't want to leave Miss Patty, but there was only time for me to save one person, and she had already lived a long and meaningless life.

The crash had depleted me of energy, so I was incapable of carrying Lana very far. "It's fine, I can walk," she said. We walked side by side to a parking lot twenty feet away from the crash site. Miss Patty slowly exited the vehicle and got on her mobile phone. We watched as she hobbled to the side of the road. Lana thought she was injured due to the impeded way she was walking; I assured sweet Lana that Miss Patty always walked as though both her ankles were broken.

A firetruck, an ambulance, and a police car arrived on the scene. Miss Patty attempted to speak with one of the officers; I knew it was a terrible idea.

I jogged over to them and introduced myself saying, "I'm ex-chief of police of the Michigan State police force Jeremy Jude. What do we have here?"

Miss Patty yelled at me to go back to the parking lot. "Stand down, civilian!" I commanded, looking her in the eyes. Miss Patty clenched her fist as though contemplating swinging at my face. I was ready for her, but the officer requested that I not escalate the situation. Though he was belts below my rank, he was still a fellow officer; I decided it best to help him feel as in control of the situation as possible.

I returned to Lana full of vigor due to my interactions with my fellow officer.

"What did you say to make Miss Patty so upset?" she asked.

I explained that Miss Patty was always upset, but it was not evident most of the time because she usually buried her anger deep inside a gallon of Häagen-Dazs ice cream.

"That's not very nice," said Lana sweetly.

I looked at her beautiful, naive face and said,

"But it is humanity. All people need their Häagen-Dazs. For some it's Captain Morgan, for others it's the Trojan men, and still for some it's a woman named ecstasy. Life is the hardest part about living. Needing a Häagen-Dazs to cope makes no one terrible or unlovable; Only human."

Lana remained looking at me, and for the first time I considered the theory about eyes being windows to the soul. The theory is one reason I will never get laser eye surgery. Before Lana said another word, I jogged to a fast food joint in the parking lot.

A few minutes later I returned with two ice cream cones to celebrate us not dying in a car crash. I thought of buying one for Miss Patty, but I realized she had been dead on the inside for years.

"But it's freezing out here," explained Lana, reluctantly taking the cone from my hand.

I held my cone up to the air and said, "Look. What do you see?"

She shrugged.

"Ice cream doesn't melt in the cold, making it the most reasonable time to indulge in the treat."

Lana smiled at my reasoning and bit directly into the ice cream; I cringed.

"That doesn't hurt your teeth?" I asked.

"No, it never has; I don't know why." She bit it again, and I marveled.

It doesn't take a genius to know everyone loves ice cream, but it does take a genius to "carpe" the "diem" and give some tangible ice cream to such an awe-inspiring girl. We ate our ice cream together as we gazed at the scenery of the totaled car ascending onto a tow truck, sunlight reflecting off the green paint so that it almost looked appealing. I am always astonished at how a normal day can turn into a rather overwhelmingly beautiful experience.

Lana and I lived exactly 2.3 miles from one another. We were approximately four miles from Lana's house. I asked her if she wanted to walk home with me, to which she replied, "I don't know…we might have to wait on the police."

Most humans interpret an "I don't know" to actually mean that the person does not know; my gifted mind allows me to see past the words to the true meaning: "Convince me, please!" I explained to Lana that I knew the back way to her house, as I'd been there before with my mom; It was a safe route with little traffic. I reminded her that both our parents were at work, and it would take a while for the police to take us home. (I also wanted to leave before any officers asked for my testimony; I didn't want to get Miss Patty arrested for reckless driving.) My convincing worked.

"Okay," said Lana, "but we can't just walk away. They'll stop us."

I yelled to my fellow officer, "Officer, I'm escorting this lady to the restroom! Don't worry, she's in good hands!" Miss Patty watched from the distance as we entered the fast food joint from the east side; We waited a minute then walked out the door from the west side of the building.

As we sauntered down the sidewalks of an upscale neighborhood, I noticed Lana had begun to shiver like a cold dog. She had left her coat in the now-towed car. I offered her my coat, and she accepted with a grin and her familiar ruddy cheeks. I wanted to pinch those cheeks, but decided it would have been hypocritical since I hated when my aunt did this to me.

There was once a study conducted on altruistic behavior with results concluding that humans never do anything that does not benefit them in some way. In other words, it is impossible for a human to be entirely selfless. This study was confirmed to me when I realized my reason for giving Lana my coat was to make her think I was a caring gentleman. I was now freezing, but not in an entirely unbeneficial way.

I wish I could say that Lana's beautiful appearance was all the warmth I needed on that walk, but her looks had no effect on my body temperature whatsoever. If anything, she was likely making me feel colder; blood pressure drops slightly in males when they are even partially aroused. Lana and I walked in silence for the most part. I appreciated her rare ability as a woman to not constantly say words. On occasion, she would ask what I was thinking; this gave me the opportunity to thoroughly explain my theory about amnesia patients never experiencing deja vu.

Two and a half hours later we arrived at Lana's house. I noticed her yard was covered in leaves. "You don't hide in leaf piles, Lana, do you?" I asked with mild concern. I told her of the terrible stories of children being run over by cars while hiding in such piles. Lana was horrified, but at least now I was sure she would never attempt to scare me by hiding in a pile of leaves.

"Well...thanks for walking me home," said Lana. As she turned to leave, I showed her the gold necklace in my hand. "Oh, I almost forgot. You dropped this in the car," I explained. Before I could say anything more, she snatched the necklace from me.

"Oh my god, thank you!" she exclaimed. "I didn't even notice it fell! I'd just die if it got lost!"

The necklace hadn't really fallen off her neck; truthfully, I had stolen it from her while carrying her from the burning vehicle. She had mentioned it being her grandmother's in class, so I knew it was important to her. It wasn't easy undoing the necklace with one hand while carrying her in my arms, but it helped that she had still been in shock from the crash. I thought the necklace might be useful for future appearances of altruism, I was correct.

I held out my hand for the necklace again. "May I?" I asked, indicating that I could help her place the necklace around her neck. She nodded, and we locked eyes as I reached my hands around her neck to fasten the necklace. Never had I watched another person's pupils dilate; it was eerie but luring.

Once the necklace was fastened, I let my arms linger around her. We stood in her driveway together in silence, both breathing heavily. It was just us, the breeze, and a couple of pervy birds watching from the trees above. The air around us was blue with the twilight, and strands of Lana's hair twirled delicately around her face. It crossed my mind that if we ever had children, there was a high probability that they would be gifted like me. How would a normal person like Lana be able to handle living in a house of anomalies? I didn't care; I leaned in and kissed her beautiful mouth.

We kissed for several minutes. I now knew what it would feel like if I were her toothbrush. I had become so accustomed to my own tongue being in my mouth that I was surprised to learn how foreign the texture of another human's tongue felt. At times I would attempt to kiss her cheek as a sort of palate cleanser, but she would unintentionally stop me with her mouth. It was passionate to the point that I feared accidentally biting her tongue off; in the heat of the moment, it seemed extremely possible. After a while, she stepped back.

"My parents aren't home," she practically whispered. It was an odd thing for her to say at that moment, but I told her not to worry. Perhaps all our kissing had made her miss her parents' affection.

"They'll be here in an hour," I reminded her comfortingly. She nodded awkwardly and kissed me on the cheek goodbye.

The walk to my house was intense, mostly due to the fact that Lana still had my coat. I was shivering to the point that my legs ached. My groinal area throbbed due to the freezing temperature; it was the first time cold weather left me with a temporary limp. Regardless of the pain, I had never felt better. How could it be that the mere touch of another person could alter emotional worlds? I was baffled by Lana's strange abilities to bite ice cream and to so easily affect me. The mouth-to-mouth interaction between Lana and me also left me with numerous questions about a subject that is often taboo in society, but is too important to be left unaddressed. Soon, I would find my answers.

CHAPTER 5: SEX AND FATHERHOOD

"I've never seen a bird and a bee having intercourse. It must be a
horrific experience for the bird."
—Jeremy Jude

Bowling makes me feel sad. I've never seen a modern or even remotely sanitary bowling alley. They all suffer from the same buzzing fluorescent lights, mildewed carpet, and the distinct smell of stale popcorn and cigarettes. I once observed a sheriff sitting at a table in a bowling alley with four empty cups of beer and an open gun holster. I never saw him bowl. I thought about taking his gun, but I decided he would need it to get to the parking lot without being killed.

It was Lana's idea to go bowling; I went along with it only for her sake. She said she wanted us to celebrate our newly obtained driver's licenses and our two months of being boyfriend and girlfriend. How knocking down pins with a heavy ball is symbolic of romantic relationships, I'll never know, but I suppose only gifted minds require meaning in everything.

After an intensely competitive game of bowling, I took Lana to a small Chinese restaurant I used to own as a child. Afterwards, we kissed each other passionately in her car. We had improved our technique since the initial tooth-brushing experience. I much preferred it to bowling.

At school the next day, there was an assembly for junior high and high school students—a crash course on sex education. Though I was already enrolled in a health class, the assembly would be beneficial, as our health teacher was heavily religious and skipped most of the chapters on sexual health. I assumed it was the nine recent unplanned pregnancies in the school that brought about this similarly unplanned assembly. I had been told early on that my services as a school principal were "not wanted," so I simply stood back and allowed the iceberg to hit the ship.

A woman stood before the 826 students in silence until all the chattering voices in the crowd subsided. She introduced herself as a practicing physician but said she preferred to be called Liz. She was dominant like Castro, yet kind like pre-communist Guevarra. Liz began talking about the basic anatomy of a female. She mentioned that women, on average, have more body fat than men, which means they are more able to survive in extremely cold temperatures. The female breast is composed entirely of fat, unless it is a synthetic breast, in which case it is composed of silly cones. This brings about the question of why men don't have breasts. Perhaps Mother Nature was tired of men having all the physical advantages, which makes me wonder if Mother Nature is a second-wave feminist. Also, does Mother Nature even exist? The point being, when I fell into my neighbors pool last winter, I got hypothermia. I could have really used a warm pair of breasts at that moment. They could have saved my life if I had died that day.

According to the doctoress, a female can tell she is pregnant if she vomits and no longer uses periods in her writing. I wondered what it meant when a male throws up. Why aren't men able to be with child? To wait on one person to create multiple children seems inefficient. Imagine the beauty of husband and wife being pregnant at the same time. The husband would no longer need to pretend to understand a pregnant woman's needs. And again, if men had breasts they could take turns breastfeeding. Granted, the earth would move toward overpopulation at twice the rate, but fathers would be more involved in raising their children since they would have to experience the agony of childbirth.

Most humans are apprehensive about thought processes like this one, but as a genius, my need to question everything is stronger than my fear of destroying my own perceptions of the world. For example, I once questioned the idea of combining peanut butter and jelly. To this day, I feel unethical eating a PB and J. Do I miss the sandwich? Yes, every day, but it's the cost of being a true existentialist.

Liz concluded the assembly by emphasizing the importance of using condoms. She explained that condoms prevent the spread of STD's, HIV's, and babies. She passed a bucket full of condoms around to all the students. Several guys inflated their condoms like balloons; these were likely the fathers of the nine school babies. I grabbed a handful of condoms and stuffed them into my pockets. I took more than I personally needed, but I planned on passing them around to the students I knew would make terrible parents.

When the first time machine is invented, I will start a charity dedicated to sending thousands of condoms to the parents of babies that grew up to be horrible humans. Perhaps if someone had given Vlad Dracula's parents a condom, no one in his village would have been impaled. Then again, I'm not sure condoms existed in the 1400's. In that case, HIV may have been a better son to them than Vlad.

Later that evening, I called Lana to ask her what she thought about males having breasts. She told me she couldn't wrap her head around the idea, as she had been vomiting the night before and still didn't feel quite like herself. It occurred to me that we had made out in her car without condoms.

"Oh my god… are you're pregnant?" I asked.

Poor Lana chuckled weakly and blamed her upset stomach on the food we'd eaten at my restaurant after bowling.

"That's illogical, Lana," I said. I'd always kept the place up to code. Many people assume it is impossible to impregnate a girl with a simple kiss, but how do you think the Virgin Mary got pregnant? Also, wouldn't it make sense that of all people, *I* would be the victim of such a rare phenomenon? There was simply too much evidence stacked against the obvious conclusion.

I decided not to push the pregnancy issue. Lana needed space to be able to accept her pregnancy in her own time. While I waited for her to come to terms with her pregnancy, I decided to prepare myself for fatherhood. The next day, I sacrificed attending class to join an elementary school's recess. It was important for me to try to connect with a young child, preferably one that looked like a mix between Lana and me.

Once on the playground, I scanned the area for an ideal practice son. I approached a small boy with dark hair and freckles and asked if he wanted to play catch with me. He agreed, and I showed him the baseball I had under my hat. He was terrible at catch for a six-year-old, but he was my son for the day, and I was proud of him for trying. I told him to feel free to share anything on his mind; he said Elizabeth K. was eating paper earlier. I asked what kind of paper, but he just shrugged. I told him to find out and get back to me.

Soon another boy wanted to play catch with us. It was still plausible that Lana and I could be having twins, so I adopted him for extra practice. He was better at catch than my first son, but I pretended to love them both equally. We all laughed every time the ball hit the ground. It was one of the best days I've ever had.

The fun was disrupted when an elderly, rigid teacher approached me and told me I wasn't allowed to be on the school grounds.

"Just let me say goodbye," I begged the horrible woman. Her fists were digging into her hips, and it occurred to me that she might want to use those fists on me. I leaned in quickly to kiss my children on the forehead, but they sprinted back across the playground as if they didn't even know me. Of course, I had probably embarrassed them in front of their friends. Being a father is a thankless job, but I found it extremely gratifying.

"Hey son!" I yelled out to my favorite son. He turned to me. For a second I paused, then I threw him the baseball. I admit, I overestimated my child's ability to catch a fastball. Walking away from my son when he was in tears with his hands covering his little bloody nose was difficult, but I knew it would only make him tougher. Besides, the horrible teacher was again yelling, and in my direction. I thought it best to leave before she embarrassed herself in front of the children.

Realizing I was getting ahead of myself, I went to a lamaze class to prepare myself for Lana's birth. All the women around me were pregnant with babies. I was pregnant, too, with anticipation. By the end of the class, I felt more prepared to breathe properly on Lana's big day, but I was still unable to fully grasp what it meant to be a father.

A few days later, in health class, a video trying to scare adolescents out of engaging in sexual behaviors was being played on the projector. I was pondering what could be the best way to raise my child. The screams coming from the video of a woman giving birth made it difficult to brainstorm. I raised my hand and asked the sex teacher if we could watch a video of a pregnant woman with an epidural giving birth instead, but he ignored me.

After the video, the teacher pulled a cart full of baby dolls from the closet. I assumed it was his own personal collection. He explained that they were expensive dolls programmed to cry at random times, just as a real baby would. I was relieved when he explained that the dolls belonged to the school district.

Our assignment was to take care of one of these dolls for a week with a classmate of the opposite sex. The teacher paired me with June, who was often considered the most attractive girl in class. Blonde hair and grayish-blue eyes have never been traits I associate with beauty, but she managed to pull it off okay. As we waited in line together to get our baby, June smiled at me and said, "I hope our baby's as attractive as its father." I hoped the same, so I was disappointed that the baby we got had its mother's features. I should have known June would have the dominant genes.

"So, what should we name it?" she asked.

I told her she should come up with the name; I was more concerned with naming Lana's and my baby.

"Let's name him Charlie!" she said gleefully. I agreed to the name, even though I couldn't think of a single genius in history with the name Charlie. June invited me to her house after school to put in our mandatory hours with Charlie. I told her I'd be there. She kissed me on the cheek slowly and walked out of the classroom with my baby. She was already taking her role of "wife" very seriously. A male student nudged me and winked on his way out. I winked back at him and said, "Fatherhood, right?" at which point we were both a little confused.

That afternoon, I talked with Lana on the phone as I drove to June's house. At one point I asked Lana how she was feeling. She claimed she felt fine. I reminded her to avoid caffeine.

"Why do I need to avoid caffeine?" she asked, and I realized she still hadn't come to terms with her pregnancy.

"Because caffeine is the equivalent of watered-down cocaine." I replied, cleverly covering up my real intentions. Lana started saying something about cocaine, but I didn't get to hear the rest.

At that moment, I saw a slender hand knocking on my driver's side window. I jolted; I thought an officer had seen me drive through the four red lights. Then I realized I had already parked in June's driveway, and it was only her hand knocking.

"Lana, I have to go. My wife and baby need me right now."

"What?" Lana said. I deduced that she was confused by my statement. I clarified that it was not a real wife and baby but that I was spending the afternoon at a girl's house pretending to be married to her. Lana asked me if I was being serious.

"Oh yes, very serious. This performance has to be believable," I explained. She seemed upset about something. Perhaps the topic of parenthood was making her face the truth of her own pregnancy. She needed space, so I hung up the phone and rolled down my window.

"Hey, you!" said June, as though she had known me for years. If she really wanted to play the role of a married couple with a baby it would take more than a kiss on the cheek and a "Hey, you." Still, I appreciated her efforts and decided to play along as realistically as possible. "Where's Charlie?" I asked in my best caring father/loving husband tone.

June pulled me into her house and led me to the living room where Baby Charlie was sound asleep on the couch.

"Did you feed him?" I asked. She smiled as though I had said something witty. I knew our baby didn't have a stomach, but I was committed to my role.

Rain began to pour from the sky. Soon there was thunder. It must have awoken the baby, because he began to cry in his distinguishably mechanical voice. June picked him up and began to rock him. (There was a sensor inside Charlie that, when tilted back and forth, comforted him.) I was very impressed with June's thin but shapely physique. One would never guess she was a mother. Watching her rock our baby back and forth made me feel like a very lucky man.

Charlie finally stopped crying. June, next to me on the couch with Charlie asleep in her arms, whispered, "Let's go up to my room to put Charlie to bed. Want to?" I told her we needed to stay near Charlie while he slept; I had yet to buy a baby monitor and could not risk our baby getting SIDS.

June seemed unusually eager to spend time with Baby Charlie in her room. She grabbed my hand and led me upstairs to her room. The thunder and rain increased, but Charlie remained sound asleep. I wondered if the baby Lana and I were going to have would be as well-behaved as Baby Charlie. June crept over to the door and slowly locked it. She turned to me and whispered, "My parents won't be home for hours." This is the same thing Lana said to me the first time we kissed. Why do girls worry about their parents' location when in the company of a genius?

The thunder and rain outside had increased; I could see rain and trees blowing as lightning flashed, outlining June's silhouette as she walked toward me from the door. She was breathing more heavily than usual.

"Are you okay, dear?" I asked in a husbandly manner. She sat close to me on the bed and softly whispered in my ear, "You wanna do this?" It was a vague inquiry, but I deduced she was referring to Charlie's vaccinations.

"Of course, darling!" I replied with supportive inflection.

June was committed to the role of being my spouse, perhaps to a fault. She began unbuttoning her pants in front of me as if she were a wife deprived of intimacy in a troubled marriage. It was a brilliant character choice! I decided to play along.

"Oh, not tonight, dear," I said. "I've had a long day at work. Besides, you know we can't afford another baby!" She feigned disappointment. I got goose chills. This was no longer just a school assignment; this was art. It was the kind of strange, abstract, raw art that only brilliant minds could discover. Was June a savant like me? Time would show that she was not.

The next day after school, I took Lana to a rather inexpensive buffet. My main motive in taking her to this place was the unlimited chocolate fountain. Lana seemed upset the last time we spoke, and chocolate is the most helpful substance to a woman. The lack of sweetness in a downtrodden female is replaced by the sweetness of the chocolate. Sadly, the liquid chocolate had no effect on her; she only ate salad. I encouraged her to eat more because she was eating for two.

"That's not funny," she said sternly. We sat in silence for most of the meal; it was pleasant.

"Okay, Jeremy, I need to say something," she began, breaking the nice silence. I put down my tapioca and looked into her eyes. (Eye contact is a commonly used technique by humans to give the illusion of emotional understanding.) She began her divulgence: "I know I probably have nothing to worry about, but I've been feeling uncomfortable about you and that girl spending time alone in her house." I reached out and grabbed Lana's hand. (Physical touch is a commonly used technique to give the illusion of love and support).

"Darling, June and I are safe," I said reassuringly. "If anything were to happen, the neighbors are always nearby, and the police are just a phone call away."

"Jeremy, I'm worried June wants to have sex with you, okay?"

I slowly took a bite of my tapioca. "It needs more sugar, I think," I explained as I poured a fourth packet of sugar into my bowl.

"Are you listening to me?" she asked.

"What'd you say?" I replied. Even the way she frowned was adorable.

"I need more salad," she said as she stormed off towards the food.

Life is about reading between the lines. Lana was actually saying that she was envious of the family I had with June and Baby Charlie. If Lana would have only accepted her own pregnant state, I could have explained to her that the family I was going to have with her and Baby Alan was much more important to me than my pretend family. Our meal returned to silence, only now it felt just a little less pleasant.

Two days later, June and I were spending quality time with Baby Charlie on her parents' porch. The afternoon sun was shining bright. June decided she wanted to tan, so she put on a bikini and lay out on the porch floor at my feet, almost as a dog would. The porch seemed like an odd place to tan since the roof blocked most of the sun, but part of being a good husband is learning not to argue with your wife's illogical decisions. I thought Charlie might benefit from a little more color, too; I wanted to ensure that he would develop his old man's complexion. He already looked too much like his pale mother, and I slightly despised June for it. I set him in the corner of the porch where a patch of sunlight beamed down on his baby face.

June lay face down on a towel and asked me to untie her bikini top; she was worried about the strap being burned by the sun. I was comfortable sitting on the porch steps and was beginning to realize that being a husband was a lot of work. I asked Baby Charlie to help June, but he just stared at me blankly. I moved over to June and untied her bikini top when a furious woman's voice yelled out, "Are you kidding me!?" It was Lana. She was walking towards us from the sidewalk, glaring more with every step.

June quickly stood to her feet, holding onto her top with both hands.

"Jeremy, what the hell are you doing!?" asked Lana, brimming with curiosity.

"Who is this?" asked my wife with intrigue.

"Is life just an illusion?" I asked, completing the triad of inquiries.

I swept Baby Charlie up into my arms as he began to weep uncontrollably. I am still not sure whether he was distraught by all the questions or whether his crying mechanism had simply been set off by the column I had accidentally struck his face on. June and Lana stared at me with slight concern.

"He'll be fine," I explained.

Lana proceeded to ask questions about what June and I were

doing; I tried to explain again that I had been spending time with my family, but it seemed to add to the confusion, so I kept silent. As I watched my wife (June) and my future wife (Lana) argue on the porch, I realized Baby Charlie deserved better. I wrapped Charlie in my arms and swiftly carried him down the porch steps and across the yard. Behind me I heard Lana and June grow silent. I walked several miles with my sweet baby in hand until reaching my destination. There are some things a man should never have to endure in his life, and I was about to endure one of them.

The next day in health class, our teacher asked for us to bring our babies forward so he could plug them into his computer and track how nurturing we were being to them. "Okay, uh, June and Jeremy. Oh look, two J's! Let's call you the 'J' team," mumbled the sex teacher in attempts to be cool. My heart was heavy. I hadn't talked to June since taking Charlie away the night before. She looked over at me to see if I had baby Charlie; I didn't.

I stood to my feet and somberly addressed the teacher. "Professor Sex," I began.

"Don't call me that," he said. I continued.

"June and I are unable to bring our baby forward. Last night it was made clear to me that Baby Charlie was being raised in a chaotic and confusing environment. As a father, I realized my baby deserves a better life than the one June, Lana, and myself can offer him. As a result, I have painfully decided to put Baby Charlie up for adoption."

After a long line of unnecessary questioning, the sex teacher finally understood that Charlie was gone for good.

The night before, I had taken him to a rail yard and thrown him onto a moving train with a note attached to his neck. The hardest part was hearing my baby's cry fade away as the train moved farther and farther down the tracks. I'm man enough to admit I shed a couple tears. I was left with nothing but the sound of a howling wind and a howling homeless man staggering away from the tracks.

(He had just jumped off the moving train and landed awkwardly on his hip.)

"That was a four hundred dollar baby!" exclaimed Captain Sex.

"Professor, you cannot put a price on babies. Also, Charlie was priceless."

Despite my protests, the teacher flunked June and me. It was not long after that when our marriage began to fall apart. It was inevitable; June and I had fallen out of love years ago. Charlie had been our last attempt to reconnect with one another. I now see that we were intellectually incompatible.

The fiasco with my first family illustrated to me that, for people with gifted minds like mine, sexual attraction isn't enough to sustain a relationship. The fiasco with Lana illustrated to me that, when a girl claims she isn't pregnant, there are extremely rare occasions where she end ups being right. It wasn't until Lana showed me a negative pregnancy test that I realized she wasn't with child. It must have been that Lana's prophecy of not being pregnant became self-fulfilled by her subconscious body. As a genius, I have learned never to underestimate the power of the mind. It can alter reality.

In the end, Lana and I remained together after a conversation in which she long-windedly expressed her frustrations about some of my preceding behaviors. I simply replied "I understand" at the various pauses in her chattering. (This is a commonly used technique to give the illusion that you understand what you did wrong.) It was nice to return to the simple life of two 16-year-olds.

All the events that took place allowed me to realize I had no desire to be a father, and I had no desire for Lana to be a mother. What I needed at that moment was time to assimilate all the theories my mind had created about sex. I needed a vacation. Coincidentally, a vacation is exactly what I would get. Candice, my sister, was getting married.

CHAPTER 6:
MY SISTER'S WEDDING
Part 1: The Flight

"I've found, through personal experience, that throwing uncooked rice at a bride is only acceptable after the wedding ceremony."
—Jeremy Jude

The Wright brothers are often given credit for inventing flight. If anyone realized they plagiarized the idea from a bird, they would have been sued by the PETA organization. And I cannot help but think that if the Wright brothers had never existed, Pearl Harbor wouldn't have happened. Fake geniuses frequently squirm their way into the hearts of our blinded society. A true genius would have never invented the airplane. It is unsafe, unpredictable, and irrational for humans to travel in. This is why I, as a genius, abstain from flying whenever possible. (I also abstain from elevators, but that is beside the point.)

There I sat on the airplane with my life dangling thousands of feet above the earth. I was annoyed that I had to sit between two people. The man in the window seat next to me was an Acidic Jew: he kept chewing on antacid tablets. The girl next to me was adorable, but I didn't feel like flirting with her. I had to focus on my best man speech, which was exceptionally difficult since I had never met my sister's fiancé. All I knew about him was that his name was Leo Martinez and that he was from Argentina. In fact, that's where this dreadful flight was taking us. At the time I knew very little about Argentina. I hoped Leo spoke English; I was on vacation and was in no mood to learn his native tongue.

"Would you care for something to drink, sir?" yelled the flight attendant. I would have fallen out of my chair had my seatbelt been unbuckled. I was irritated by her tone and decided not to interact with her. The adorable girl next to me elbowed me and whispered, "Babe, she's talking to you." Lana pointing out the obvious further annoyed me. She was flying with us because my sister needed a last-minute bridesmaid to replace the one that had been in an unexpected car crash. (I suppose all car crashes are unexpected, though.) The rest of my sister's closest friends were occupied with graduate-level courses.

While I was happy to have my girlfriend come with me, everything she said during the flight put me on edge. In fairness to her, I was already on edge, as I felt that death was always seconds away. Still, I had read in a pamphlet that Argentina could be very romantic; I thought that perhaps we would be able to make out under a canopy as the sun set.

I stared at the paper on my tray. The task of filling it with compliments about my future brother-in-law seemed daunting. I began with the following words:

> *What can I say about Leo? As we all know, "Leo" is Latin for "lion." Thus, Leo is similar to a lion, not so much in aggression, but more-so in his tan, muscular anatomy...*

I was mildly proud of what I wrote; I showed it to Lana, and she shrugged. Suddenly a horrendous odor emanated from our row. I glared at the highly Acidic Jew; he was pretending to be asleep. Not only did he discharge such an offensive odor, he let me take the blame for it. Everyone knows humans are incapable of flatulating in their sleep.

A flight attendant walked past us and noticed the toxic flavor lingering near us. She gagged at the smell, and rightfully so. I knew she was judging me. The Jewish man next to me yawned wide, and I hoped it was a wake-up yawn. It was not. I just had to sit there and accept that everyone in the cabin hated me for this man's actions. They say Jews don't eat pork, but maybe this one did.

A baby began to cry across the aisle. It brought back memories of baby Charlie being carried away by the train. I was a bundle of nerves. I grabbed my paper and pen and ran to the restroom, locking myself in. This was a poor decision. It reminded me of a coffin, which seemed all too appropriate to have in an airplane. In the shaking restroom, with my shaking hands, I somehow managed to write this nugget of silver:

> *I remember when Leo was only ten years old. He used to say there was a perfect someone out there for him. Every night he'd walk down to the local wishing well and throw a peso into the water. He always wished that, wherever his future wife was, she would be happy on that day. Of course, when his parents found out he wasted a peso, they were furious...*

While writing, I managed to pull my pants down with one hand. I sat on the toilet attempting to urinate, but I was too distraught by the slight trembling of the plane. I got up and flushed the empty toilet out of habit. It sounded as though my stall had detached from the rest of the cabin and was falling to the ground. My life flushed before my eyes.

The pilot announced there was strong turbulence and ordered us to go back to our seats. Who did he think he was? Still, I had to give him credit; he was spot-on about the turbulence. Writing my best man speech would have to be postponed. I burst out the door and sprinted down the aisle screaming as loudly as possible; screaming, I find, is a great distraction from crippling fear. It was after this moment that I realized this flight did not have an air marshal.

Back in our row, Lana sat clenching the armrests for stability. "Are you okay?" she asked me, having heard me screaming down the aisle. I could hardly breathe, much less respond. I quickly buckled my seatbelt.

"Where were you?" she asked as she grabbed my hand.

"I needed some metaphorical air," I replied, fully aware all the air in the plane was the same. A flight attendant rushed the beverage cart to the back of the plane as though it were a safety hazard. I felt bad for the people that hadn't gotten their drinks yet. If we were going to die, we all deserved one last drink.

The captain shouted over the PA system, nearly giving me a heart attack. "Folks, we're experiencing some...heavy turbulence. Nothing out of the ordinary, but we ask that you remain in your seats with your seatbelts securely fastened."

I shut my eyes tightly in preparation of my death.

"It's okay. It's just a little shaking," explained Lana as she rubbed my back gently. "We're fine, love."

I was soothed by sweet Lana until a violent shaking occurred. I saw fear in the eyes of a flight attendant, which is never a good sign. Several people in the cabin gasped. The shaking only increased in magnitude. The captain's voice resounded over the PA saying, "Flight attendants, please take your seats immediately." Lana held my hand tightly with her eyes shut.

"Are we gonna be okay?" she asked, trembling with fear.

"It's definitely unlikely in these conditions," I stated factually. In cases like these, humans are supposed to lie, but I couldn't take that risk. If in the afterlife we are punished for lying, I certainly didn't want my last sentence to be a lie.

The air reeked of fear and a lingering hint of the Acidic Jew's gastrointestinal miscarriage. Across the aisle from us was a ritzy man in his late twenties. He wore a white Lacoste polo shirt, noise-canceling headphones, a diamond-encrusted watch, and a face that only a blind mother could love. I deduced it was his parents, and not him, that were rich, since he lacked all qualities of a hard-working typhoon. The pilot asked that all electronic appliances be turned off, and the young man yelled out, "Are you serious!? This is ridiculous!" At that moment, part of me wanted the plane to crash; I was willing to make that sacrifice for mankind.

Without a fair warning from the pilot, the plane went into a freefall for five of the longest seconds of my life. Lana nearly broke my hand with her grip, and I nearly broke hers. I watched as a woman several rows in front flew out of her seat and cracked her head on the ceiling. Interestingly, no one laughed at her. Everyone was busy screaming, shouting, and generally panicking; I decided to join in on this collective activity. Then the plane suddenly leveled out as if nothing had ever happened.

The cabin was now completely silent; no one could really speak. I looked around at all the horrified faces. Poor Lana had wept during the fall. I wiped a tear from her cheek; she wiped several from mine.

Suddenly I heard the voice of a man yell out, "This airline had better pay for a new shirt!" It was the voice of the wealthy young man. A bloody Mary he had ordered earlier had spilled all over him during the freefall.

I thought long and hard of how a person could come to be someone like this wealthy boy. This man's parents were wealthy enough that, in the face of death, the man thought of nothing more than his soiled shirt. I leaned over to the man.

"How rich must one be to think of himself as immortal?" I asked him.

He scoffed at my question as he put on his Bose noise cancelling headphones. Today I understand, of course, that of all the humans in that plane, he feared death the most; he had more to lose on this earth than all the passengers combined.

"Disgusting," the Acidic Jew whispered under his breath. I turned to look at him; he was staring down at my crotch. I glared at him and said, "Oh, look who's awake!" Scanning my surroundings, I quickly deduced I was the only person who had urinated in their pants.

I glanced over at Lana, who had a horrified expression. "The storm has passed," I explained to her, which didn't seem to change her state.

In my defense, there was an element of genius to my bodily discharge. If the plane had hit the ground while I was full of water, the impact would have been greater due to the extra mass in me. The urinary discharge hypothetically saved my life.

I leaned towards the Jewish man and said, "At least I didn't let you take the blame for my urination as you'd let me take the blame for your gasses."

He shook his head and leaned against the window, pretending to be asleep again. I cleverly leaned back in my chair and pretended to sleep as well. I hoped, this time, the flight attendants would blame him for my soaking wet pants.

CHAPTER 6:
MY SISTER'S WEDDING
Part 2: Leo Martinez

We landed in Buenos Aires, Argentina, several hours later with no more incidents, other than the occasional glare from the Acidic Jew. After getting through customs, Lana and I met with my parents, who had sat in the back of the plane. So far the country seemed lovely, but it was too early to tell. Judging a country by its airport is like judging a book by its cover: while the cover is usually a strong indicator of the rest of the book, there are exceptions to the rule. As we waited for our bags in the baggage claim area, I pulled the best man speech out of my pocket and wrote:

> *I'll be honest, when my sister told me she was marrying an Argentine human, the first thing that came to mind was the Falklands War. I feared the tension between Argentines and United Statesians would be too much for our families to overcome. Then I remembered the war primarily involved the British. Granted, Miss Thatcher was in direct communication with the United States at the time, but it was mostly small talk. The point being, Leo, if you hurt my sister, I will end who you are...*

It ended up being the more aggressive part of my speech, but it was essential for me to let my heart flow through the pen.

My inspiration was suddenly interrupted by my sister's screeching voice. "Oh my gooosh! Look how tall you are! Is this your girlfriend?"

As I stood to give the obligatory greeting, Lana and Candice hugged in that classic "I-don't-want-you-to-hate-me" way. It was sweet.

Behind Candice stood a suave lion of a man named Leo Martinez. Muscular, tan, and towering over the rest of us, he looked exactly as I had pictured him based on the picture my mother had shown me of him. He extended his hand for me to shake; I was concerned he would fail to realize his own strength and something awful would happen to my bones.

"No thanks," I said, giving him a thumbs up instead.

My dad reached out and shook his hand; Leo leaned in and kissed my dad on the cheek. I deduced this cheek kissing was part of Leo's culture, but I thought of how easy it would be for Leo to get away with anything at that moment. If he had kissed my mother on the mouth with enough nonchalance, the rest of us would have just stood there and accepted it as part of his culture.

We watched as Leo chased down every single piece of luggage we asked him to; it was a sight to see. I admired his statuesque physique to the point that I feared Lana would be jealous if she knew my inner thoughts. This man did everything with a "no problem" attitude. I became painfully aware that we were living up to the stereotype(s) of United Statesians being out of shape and/or owning slaves. Be that as it may, I had just gotten off a long flight and was in no mood to collect my own things.

We stood and watched like tourists as Leo single-handedly put our things in the back of the large, white rental van. (To clarify, when I say "single-handedly" I mean unassisted; he did use both hands.) Leo hopped into the driver's seat, and the rest of us followed into the van. As the van careened down the busy, five-lane highway I concluded that our chances of perishing in that van were one in five. I'm not a pessimist; the genius brain makes these calculations automatically.

A man in a faded red sedan next to us signaled for Leo to roll down his window. The man pointed at Lana and yelled something through the highway wind. Leo shook his head and rolled up the window. I asked Leo what the man wanted. Leo explained that the man wanted to take Lana with him in his car. I wondered if this was common practice in Argentina. Either way, it seemed like a very impractical way of asking a girl out. What happens when she says yes? Must she jump onto the moving vehicle? Perhaps it is how love is tested in this country. It isn't my place to judge.

As we got farther into the city, the traffic thickened. All the air in Buenos Aires smelled faintly like cigarette smoke; I eventually became addicted to the smell. We witnessed an impatient bus squeeze between our lane and the parked cars by the sidewalk. It scraped a total of six cars and a cyclist. Leo shook his head in disgust; the rest of us refrained from commenting on the incident for fear of seeming like judgmental United Statesians.

Downtown Buenos Aires was unexpectedly high fashion. The billboards and stores were extremely modern. It was reminiscent of parts of New York City. Many of the women we drove past looked like models. I mentioned this to Lana, but she didn't hear me. I took Lana's silence as another opportunity to add to the best man speech.

Every blue moon, we meet that special someone that takes our breath away. Leo, I am vulnerably admitting to you now, in front of all these people, that when we met I was finding it slightly difficult to breathe. In part it was because of the altitude change, but mostly it was because I thought a Greek statue had turned to flesh and bone to marry my sister. You are a phenomenon...

Of course, I was also a phenomenon, but Leo was the bronze to my brain. If by some miracle Leo and I had a baby with his looks and my brains and my looks, we would almost obligatorily have to name the child Superman.

We arrived in front of a twelve-story building. Candice explained that this was where we were staying, and that Leo's family was coming for dinner in a few hours. I wondered how all six of us would fit into a tiny apartment. I thought it would be similar to a Japanese apartment where fifteen Japanese men sleep in a closet on top of each other.

To my surprise, Leo lived in a penthouse on the twelfth floor; rather, the entire twelfth floor was his penthouse. Upon entering, we saw a grand piano atop quality wooden floors. The sofas were leather, and the counters were marble. Something was off. It is rumored that many members of the Italian mafia migrated to Argentina during World War II. I deduced that Leo Martinez was head of the Argentine mafia, which explained his wealth.

"Oh, shit! I forgot something in the van!" I yelled at the top of my lungs. My mother asked me to use less crude language. I ignored her momentarily to ask Lana to come with me; I needed to tell her the truth about who Leo truly was. Unfortunately, Leo claimed he had to come with us to enter the code for the garage. Lana and Leo made friendly small talk on the elevator ride, but I was completely silent. When we got to the van I yelled, "Oh, shit! The thing I forgot is actually in my carry on upstairs!"

Leo laughed and said, "You're so funny, man!" I knew better than to trust him. I was beginning to regret being his best man.

Within the hour, his entire family showed up with food—two parents, three siblings, three sets of aunts and uncles, and about eight cousins, some with their children. There was an intense amount of cheek kissing going on. I grabbed Lana and kissed her on the mouth repeatedly as if she were the main person I wanted to greet. No one bothered us.

We sat at the large table to eat. Everyone was talking loudly, reaching for bread, waving their hands wildly, and laughing excessively. During the course of the meal, Leo's father explained that they owned an international chocolate brand, the name of which I didn't care to memorize. I knew it was common practice for mafia members to work in the food industry, and a chocolate business seemed like an especially clever cover-up. The most known mafia leader, Al Cappuccino, owned several coffee shops in his area. They even named a cup of coffee after him called "cup of Joe." (I don't know why they chose Joe, though, since Al was his name.)

As I watched Leo and his family at the table, I realized I had misjudged them. Had they murdered people? Undoubtedly, yes, but I'm sure they were all justified murders. Leo was on the good side of the mafia, and I knew Candice would be safe in the arms of this rugged beast. I was so inspired, I took out my paper and wrote:

> *I recently found out that Leo's family owns a chocolate company. I finally understand why Leo's so sweet. My sister, Candice, has a Master's degree in chemistry, but you don't need a degree to notice the chemistry between these two...*

It was pure gold coming out of that pen! Unfortunately, I was thrown off by Leo's aunt Alejandra asking Lana if we were engaged yet. I overheard Lana explain that we were only sixteen. Aunt Alejandra said she had gotten engaged when she was only sixteen and had had a happy marriage. I wondered if Leo's aunt was onto something and gazed over at Lana. I caught my reflection in her eyes, and for the first time, I could see myself with her.

CHAPTER 6:
MY SISTER'S WEDDING
Part 3: The Rehearsal

"The term 'hooking up' means different things in our society,
depending on the type of intercourse."
-Jeremy Jude

I awoke at 4:00 AM due to the time difference and couldn't get back to sleep, so I went to Lana's room to see if she was awake. When I knocked on her door, she opened it slowly.

"Are you awake?" I asked.

"How do you think I opened the door?" She said with a smile.

"You might be a sleepwalker. I won't jump to conclusions," I reasoned.

She chuckled. "You couldn't sleep either, huh?"

"No," I replied as I stumbled into the darkness of her room towards a window.

"What are you doing?" she asked. I pulled the window's blinds open.

"The stars will help you sleep," I explained as I began to walk back out of her room.

"Want to stay for a little while?" she asked. I accepted her offer, as lying awake with her seemed like a much better option than lying awake by myself.

We lay down in her bed and stared out at the barely visible stars. "Did you know the Milky Way isn't made from any form of dairy?" I asked.

"Yeah…"

"Good…you're smarter than most girls."

I remember Lana slowly wrapping her arms around my torso.

"Interesting…" I mused out loud. Up until that moment, the only kind of physical contact I had enjoyed was making out (with girls) or punching (guys).

"What's interesting?" She asked. I didn't answer. I could feel her again having an unusual effect on me and I wanted to immerse myself in her.

The next morning, I awoke to a knock at my room door. I noticed Lana was in bed with her arms wrapped around me, and it occurred to me that I was still in Lana's room.

There was another knock at the door; this time Lana opened her eyes. She saw my face and sat up energetically. I was happy to see her too, I suppose. She seemed nervous to answer the door, so I got up and opened the door on her behalf. My lawyer dad stood there speechless.

"Buenos dias," I said rather colloquially.

"Your mother and I have been looking for you. Why are you in Lana's room?" He asked in the typical monotone voice of a lawyer.

"We slept together," I shrugged. He hollered for my mother and told her the same information I had just shared with him. She walked over to the doorway to confirm with me that my father's information was correct; I assured her it was. Soon Candice was at the doorway asking questions, which my father impatiently answered. Lana jumped out of bed and added that we were "just talking" and we "dozed off." For whatever reason, my lawyer dad seemed to take Lana's explanation to be more pertinent than mine. The odd deposition with him ended just like that.

My mother, however, sat us down for a long conversation. "I know you're both getting to that age where you feel like exploring," she said. "All I ask is that you not explore in places where it is disrespectful to others, like Leo's home. And I suggest you just not explore too much until you're married, okay?"

I don't understand why my mother considered it disrespectful to explore the room Lana was staying in; I found nothing of interest in any of Leo's drawers. I was also surprised at how tolerant my mother seemed about Lana and me getting married.

By 7:42 that morning, we were all clumped together in the white van as Leo drove us downtown. He narrated the history of nearly every building we drove past. After a short while, I covered my ears so as not to hear him. I wasn't being rude. Being a genius, I retain everything I see and hear. The last thing I needed in my brain was an archive of aged Argentine buildings.

Leo parallel parked like a champ; I clapped loudly for him until Lana begged me to stop. We got out in front of an enormous cathedral. It resembled the cathedral that the hideous man with a hump on his back used to dwell in. The Martinez family had rented the building for the week, another strong coverup. No one would expect to find a mafia family in a church. Then again, there must be some religious reason that mafia leaders are referred to as godfathers.

The ceiling of the cathedral was approximately 254.3716 feet tall; that's a rough estimation from visual memory of the cathedral as it stood fourteen years ago. It was rounded at the top, so even a whisper could be carried across the cathedral. Undoubtedly, when people prayed, their voices traveled to another person praying; I wondered how many times people in the cathedral had heard another person praying and thought it was the voice of God.

As we entered the cathedral, Leo's parents greeted us via cheek kissing. In the entrance was a fifteenth-century version of a sink, filled with crystal clear water. Leo approached the sink and dipped his fingers in the water, running them across his forehead gently. He probably had a headache from the drive. I was still trying to wake up for the day. I approached the sink and began to wash my face thoroughly. It was refreshing. A few bystanders in the cathedral gasped, as did Leo's parents. This is when I came to the realization that I had made a mistake: the sink was for the Martinez mafia members only.

There was a long, drawn-out silence echoing across the cathedral. I heard a man in the distance sneeze, and I was tempted to laugh but knew I had to hold it together somehow. This was the decision-making silence that would make or break my bones.

Candice finally broke the silence, saying, "That's holy water, Jeremy. It's for religious purposes only." I winced. My own sister was covering up for them now. I decided to play along in order to spare my life.

"Oh, wow! I'm so embarrassed!" I exclaimed, faking the feeling of embarrassment. Leo assured me it was okay, and his parents gave off a slight chuckle. I let out a sigh of relief. I had nearly been killed in a church, which I found ironic since a church is a place where people go to hear stories about a man that had escaped death. I felt grimly spiritual at that moment.

As Candice, Leo, and their parents discussed wedding ceremony preparations, Lana and I explored the cathedral. We sauntered, hand in hand, through the halls. I was beginning to notice

Catholics' love of art. The walls were covered in stone carvings of random people. There were paintings on the ceilings of semi-nude women holding fully nude babies. Perhaps Woodstock had its origins in the Catholic art movement. I was impressed a religious organization could be so avant-garde.

Lana asked me if I believed in God. "Sure," was my response. "He can do anything he puts his mind to."

Lana laughed, and I'm still unsure why. Perhaps she felt I was being too optimistic about him, but I tend to believe all people are capable of doing amazing things. I asked her if she believed in god. "I don't know yet," was her ambiguous reply.

"Why don't you know?" I asked.

"I think I believe in god...but I've never really asked myself why I believe..." There were a few more words she said after this, but I was distracted by a nude painting behind her.

Lana walked ahead of me when she noticed a large stained glass window. She wanted to get a better view. I found myself absolutely mesmerized by her. Her walk, her voice, her laugh, her words; everything about her rubbed me the right way. She turned to me to ask what I thought about the stained glass; she noticed my exceptional amount of staring and grew silent.

"What have you done to me?" I asked in a gentle voice. We smiled at one another with reckless abandon.

I wondered how much more integrated into my soul this girl could become. In all honesty, I am still unsure where in the body the soul is located. My father once worked with a client who had no soul. The man attempted to sue an orphanage for millions of dollars because he had twisted his ankle on their property. Perhaps his soul became inoperably damaged when he fell on the pavement; this is just speculation, of course. He may have been born without a soul in the first place.

My mother called to us from the main sanctuary. Lana and I walked down the aisle to the front where Leo and Candice stood staring at each other. Before them was a priest. By now Leo's groomsmen were all present. Undoubtedly, they were all loyal members of his gang. The bridesmaids were there as well—half Argentine, half United Statesian. My mother instructed me to stand in line with the groomsmen. She was not aware I was the best man.

We began the rehearsal. Candice walked down the center aisle towards Leo wearing casual shorts and sandals. Leo, too, was in casualwear. There was also no music. It was a wedding rehearsal, yet it lacked any cadence of a wedding. The only legitimate thing about this pathetic practice run was the priest, who was in full costume even when no one else was trying.

The priest began a marvelous speech in Latin, and I regretted not taking a day to learn the language. His speech reminded me I was far from finishing my own best man speech. I pulled out the crumpled paper from my pocket and wrote:

> *The term "lovebirds" comes from an old tale of a man and a woman in love. This couple was being held in a concentration camp with nothing but chickens. One day they decided to pluck the feathers from all the chickens to make their own wings. They found some wax and used it to glue the feathers together. The next day, they executed their escape plan. They both jumped out of a tower wearing these chicken wings. As they fell to their deaths the woman yelled out, "My love, chickens can't fly!" With his last breath the man replied, "I wish you would have communicated that to me before we..." So, Leo and Candice, as you fly through marriage together as the lovebirds that you be, always remember that communication is key...*

I got chills; I truly had no idea where the speech was heading, but it ended on a surprisingly logical note. My brain solves problems subconsciously; it's why Sudoku is no fun for me. I sit there clueless while my brain fills the empty spaces with seemingly random numbers.

I noticed a seventy-something-year-old man sitting in the front pew with his arms crossed and a jaded frown on his face. The hundreds of wrinkles around his eyes and mouth far surpassed those of an average man in his seventies; he was clearly a smoker. I was intrigued by the extreme distaste for life this gentleman conveyed. He was the only human in the room without even a slight smile.

CHAPTER 6:
MY SISTER'S WEDDING
Part 4: Love and Disillusionment

"There are too many quotes about love."
-Jeremy Jude

After the rehearsal, I watched Leo embrace the elderly man fearlessly. I took this as an opportunity to find out more about this bitter being. I, too, embraced the man. It was a regrettable decision for five reasons:

1. As I went in for the hug, the man coughed a phlegmy, smokey cough in my face.

2. Wrapping my arms around him resulted in the smell of cheap cologne, cigarettes, and body odor hovering over me for the rest of the afternoon.

3. A four-second hug was too long of a hug for this gentleman.

4. As he pushed me away, he tripped over his cane and nearly fell to the ground.

5. The man's swearing echoed across the quiet church, and all eyes

fell on us.

Once the man regained his balance and others in the room had moved on from the fiasco, Leo introduced me to the swearing man as his great uncle, Marco Martinez. Marco spoke little English, as his vocabulary was mainly pessimistic. While I found his tragic tones alluring, he didn't keep my interest for long. At the time, I only studied people with exceptional skills or intellect. One of Leo's groomsmen, an overweight Argentine version of a young Voltaire, invited all the men to a bar. I thought it would be an excellent opportunity for me to work on the best man speech and to conduct a study on the concept of inebriation.

Alcohol has a specific effect on the brains of gifted individuals. I was not stumbling or mumbling, as an average intoxicated being might do, but I could not feel my face. I also noticed a rapid decline in my academic exceptionalism. I attempted to add to the best man speech during my intoxication by writing the following:

Marco is going to be a great wife to my sister. Why? Because he has what it takes. If anyone objects to their matrimony, I swear on my mother's grave! I think if you like someone, marry them. Who the hell am I to stand in your way? Candice and Leo, just do it! You are the Adam and Eve of our family in a way. Leo, I don't give a shit that you're in the mafia. I'd take a bullet for you! Candice, don't let anything happen to this man...

A hand slammed on my paper. The hand belonged to a drunk Marco, who turned out to be a happy, talkative drunk.

"Play you chess?" he asked. I couldn't distinguish if this primitive English was due to it being his second language or due to the alcohol in his blood.

"Me no play," I answered, due to the alcohol in my blood. He pointed at his chest with vigor; I leaned in to get a closer look.

"I number one chess champion Argentina!" he said proudly. I disbelieved him until Leo confirmed it to be true. Suddenly, Marco's grouchy attitude made sense. He was one of those classic troubled geniuses, like Thomas Edison or James Dean (though James never electrocuted an elephant). These are the types of geniuses I most envy. Their brooding attitudes stem from knowing the key to life yet struggling to find the door. I needed to know what he knew.

Marco stumbled to a small table outside to suck the life out of a cigarette. I stood to join him. Standing was challenging. It was even more difficult to make it outside. With every step I took, I used anything around me as a crutch – bar stools, the door jamb, people. Some of the heads I leaned on were full of oppressive hair gel. Fortunately, their shirts served as perfect cloths. For whatever reason, I could not stop shushing people, even though most of them were not even talking. One of the groomsmen asked if I needed help. I shushed him as well, but was immediately overcome with remorse for shushing him. I hugged him for what seemed to be three minutes straight. The embrace shattered my father's and my record by three minutes.

I sat across from Marco, who kept attempting to whistle. He failed every time due to the smoke steadily emerging from his lungs. I whistled a tune for him, and he smiled. My whistling usually annoyed humans terribly, but Marco was different. He was on another level entirely. Four songs later, I became lightheaded and had to stop prematurely.

"Are you excited about the wedding!?" I shouted much, much louder than anticipated.

Marco scoffed brazenly as he lit up another cigarette.

I asked "¿Qué?" meaning "what" in his language.

Marco told me love was an illusion. He believed romance was non-existent and highly fictionalized. He said it took him three divorces to figure this out. I wondered if this was the key to life Marco possessed. What if belief in love was a logical fallacy? What if love was just made up by corporations to sell more his and hers sinks?

Immediately I thought about Lana. Perhaps both she and I had been brainwashed into enjoying every minute together. Our developing admiration and respect for each other stemmed from society's misconstruction of love, and we had fallen into the trap. Marco had opened my eyes, and I could now see how irrational it was to believe in love. The one thing geniuses are incapable of being is irrational. (Believe me, I have tried on multiple occasions.) I cringed as I saw my inevitable future without love and without Lana. I could feel beads of sweat forming thick and fast on my forehead as I struggled to inhale the heaviness of the air and, not to mention, the secondhand smoke. It was as if the temperature outside had increased by ten degrees Celsius. I peeled my shirt off and tossed it to Marco. He looked at me with concern.

I stood to my feet and yelled, "Taxi!" which is Spanish for "cab" or "taxi." A taxi driver pulled up to the curb, and I stumbled to the car. The taxi driver reached back and opened the door for me after five of my own failed attempts to grab the handle. I sprawled across his backseat and grunted loudly. The rest of this day was a string of hazy events, but I somehow ended up in downtown Buenos Aires.

I vaguely remember walking past several small vendors selling miscellaneous items on the street. I must have stolen a bracelet/t-shirt combo, because when I sobered up I had a bracelet on my wrist with "I heart Argentina" written on it and the shirt to match. I also attempted to buy a broom from a salesman enticing pedestrians to buy it by demonstrating how to sweep a sidewalk. The man wouldn't let go of the broom, though. He was the worst broom salesman I had ever encountered.

I walked into a grocery store called "Carrefour," which is Spanish for "Walmart." I exited the store some undetermined amount of time later with a large chocolate egg and a bag of milk. Never before had I drank milk from a bag. I felt like a calf sucking on a cow's teat. Let it be known that milk in Argentina tastes far better than United Statesian milk. The chocolate egg was a little less spectacular; in fact, I'd say it was average at best. After leaving Carrefour, I wandered aimlessly through the city until spotting a group of electric guitars perched in a store's window display. Before entering, I decided to put on a chocolate mustache so as to appear older. I entered and asked the store owner, who had a real mustache, if I could play one of the guitars.

"No," he said in Spanish, or possibly English with a Spanish accent. We faced each other for seven and a half seconds in silence, my eyes pleading for him to change his mind and his urging me to take my overwhelmingly gifted mind elsewhere. This was the end of our interaction. Whether out of spite, or genuine physical turmoil, I will never know, but upon exiting this man's store, I puked what tasted like a chocolatey white Russian all over his doorstep.

I felt better and worse at the same time. I walked several yards away from the shop before sitting on a curb. I watched as a nearby stray dog discovered the vomit and began to lick it up. For the first time in my life, I felt depressed; I think it was depression at least. I didn't want to jump off a bridge or spend the rest of my day crying, but I did feel a sting of hopelessness that I had not experienced before. I thought about the first time I saw Lana, and the effect she'd had on my body.

"How could I have feigned this?" I asked the scraggly mutt. None of it made sense. Marco was a chess champion, a genius among men, a royal treasure in my book, so why did his theory seem so groundless?

I wiped off my chocolate milk mustache (which had become more of a smeared goatee after my recent outpouring) and trudged to a local playground to sulk. The swings in Argentina have chains twice as long as United Statesian swings. I sat and began swinging, and as the forces of alcohol and physics swayed me, I began to forget my troubles. I swung higher and higher, until I became endowed with the belief that I could fly.

Suddenly I was no longer flying, and I felt a hard force slam into me. Apparently, swinging and drunkenness do not mix. I opened my eyes to see several Argentine humans staring at me. I was lying in the dirt nine feet from the swing I had mounted moments—or maybe years—ago. There was blood on my elbows, a gaping hole in my jeans, and immense pain throughout my body. To this day I cannot say for sure what happened, but it is likely that someone pushed me off or a gust of tornado-like wind had rushed past. Some speculate that I simply fell off the swing on my own; however, such a cause is highly improbable and therefore not being considered as a legitimate theory.

Breathing was agony. A woman called for an ambulance. As I waited on the ground with the natives, I felt a strange new sense of peace come over me. A man placed his suit jacket under my head. It smelled magnificent. I asked him what brand of cologne he wore, but he didn't speak English.

"You are too pale," said a woman in broken English, adding insult to my injury.

Paramedics arrived ten minutes and seventeen seconds later. They put me in a stretcher and carried me to the back of the ambulance. I attempted to say, "This is a little dramatic, gentlemen," but when I tried speaking, a sharp shooting pain crawled from my neck down to my anus. At the time, I was not aware that losing mobility of one's legs is usually a sign of something more severe.

One of the paramedics stuck a needle in my arm; it was connected to an IV bag filled with magic, universal love and deep contemplation. As the ambulance sped down the road, I stared up at the ceiling, drooling out of my mouth. To be honest, the drugs were not making me drool; rather, I had a deep interest in my salivary glands at that moment and craved a packet of sugar. I thought of Lana and our inevitable demise. Marco's ingenious take on love tormented my thoughts. I began to feel claustrophobic on the stretcher.

Later that night, I woke up to the smell of urine. To my left, in a bed, was an extremely skinny man with small sores all over his body. To my right was an open window. I quickly deduced that I was on the third floor of a hospital and that the smell belonged to the man next to me. He greeted me with a cool thumbs up. I yelled, "Nurse!" at the top of my lungs. It was a bad idea as this hurt my ribs terribly. Gazing down, I noticed a hard-shelled vest wrapped around my torso and a hospital gown enshrouding me. I was wearing nothing else.

At the time, I thought I had been admitted into a psych ward for attempting to kill myself by jumping off the swing. Each time the nurse entered my room, I tried to explain I had not been attempting to kill myself. If I had been attempting to do so, I would have succeeded. I am not an advocate of suicide, but it is simply a known fact that a suicidal genius is too calculated to fail at his endeavor. Besides, I was far too inebriated to successfully carry out a suicide.

I eventually became aware that the hard-shelled vest was not a straight jacket but a vest. Since most of my readers likely do not have my talented deduction skills, I will directly point out that I had fractured my spine during the fall. The injury was caused by compression on my spinal column, creating a hairline fracture. The hard vest kept my column from shifting. I discovered my condition when a bilingual doctor said these things to me in English. He asked if I had any family that needed to be contacted. I jokingly pretended to have amnesia, but I committed to the role so exceptionally well that I forgot to tell him I was joking. It would take four hours before my family found out my whereabouts. During those four hours, I ate orange-flavored jello and watched Argentine soap operas with the sick man. The episodes were surprisingly good, though the morphine in my system may have skewed my objectivity.

Leo and his fat Voltaire friend were the first recognizable faces to show up. "Your family is on the way up the elevator," said Leo. He appeared to be deeply troubled by something, but I was in no shape to comfort him. He knelt at my bedside and grabbed my hand with his own beautifully crafted hand, and I felt a manly tear form in my left eye. It was the greatest moment of the entire trip.

"What happened, man?" he asked. I needed him to see me as a man so I told him I was hit by a car.

Leo wanted to know who had let me drink so much alcohol. I told him the bartender never stopped me. I did not tell him the bartender was unaware of me taking a bottle of rum when he wasn't looking. Just then, Candice entered. When she saw me, her eyes welled with tears. Leo stood to his feet and apologized profusely. His eyes welled with tears also. They embraced each other. I was somewhat irritated by their tears; whatever they were fighting about could have waited.

Within seconds, my parents also rushed into the room. Upon seeing me, my mother instantly burst into tears just as my sister had, except with a greater, overly-worried mother intensity.

"Oh, my baby, are you alright?" she asked. It was a stupid question.

My lawyer dad didn't know what to do. He stood by the window with that stoic face, giving me an odd thumbs up; I nodded in acknowledgement. My mom went in for a gentle hug. I gently placed my hand on her forehead and told her to get lost; I believe a hug would have literally killed me at that point.

"¿Dónde está Lana?" I said in Spanish. I had learned it from the soap opera. (In English it means "Where is Lana?") They told me she had been asked to wait at Leo's penthouse in case I showed up there.

The road home seemed bumpy. As Leo drove us to the penthouse, memories flashed through my brain of my conversation with the brilliantly grumpy Marco. I had completely forgotten that my drunken endeavors had begun after I heard the theory that love was a myth. For me to accept love as truth was to completely neglect the beliefs of a fellow genius.

Leo unlocked the door to his penthouse. Lana stood in the entryway staring at my mangled body in a wheelchair. My legs had started working by now, but I had been asked not to walk around with all the drugs in my system.

"Oh my god! What happened?!" she said frantically.

"Never mind that for now, Lana," I said. "Can we talk out on the balcony?"

She nodded. My dad rolled me out to the balcony, and Lana followed.

"Do you need anything?" asked my dad. I told him I was fine, and he walked away.

"Hey, shut the door though!" I yelled at my dad. He closed both French doors.

"Lana, I spoke with a genius today," I began, "and he led me to believe something very disastrous about love." I reached out for Lana's hand. She patiently listened as I gazed into her eyes. With my intoxicated lips I whispered, "He led me to believe that whatever romance you and I have together is a lie, that we are fake. When I was drugged in the back of the ambulance, I realized how realistic some imaginary things can seem. I thought a swarm of birds built a nest on my chest." I paused at the horrific memory. "Lana, they did not." At this point I pulled out a ring I had found in my pocket with the engraving "I heart Argentina" on it.

Lana was confused. I attempted to get down on one knee, but it was pure anguish. I sat back down in my chair and said, "It took me drunkenly wandering the streets of Buenos Aires to realize Marco is not a certifiable genius as I had first believed. He was only the chess champion in Argentina...not the world. Therefore, he is capable of being wrong, and I am certain he is in this case. What you and I have remains untouched. Will you marry me?"

She glanced at the ring, then at me, and said, "Jeremy, maybe now's not the time to make any decisions, okay?"

I didn't want her to elaborate; I threw the ring over the balcony and watched as the wind symbolically carried it away. Lana seemed surprisingly surprised by my gesture, considering she basically did the same thing with my heart.

"Why did you do that?" she asked, as though it wasn't obvious. She then attempted to explain why we were too young to get married. I wasn't listening. My mind was playing out a scenario in which I jumped over the balcony in my wheelchair. It was improbable without assistance, though, and I wasn't about to ask for help.

"Please excuse me. I have to finish my best man speech for Leo," I said to her in an exceptionally mature tone. She asked if I needed anything before she went inside; I reluctantly asked her for a pen and paper.

I sat out on the balcony under the scrutiny of the harsh sun. The rays beamed onto my bare arms and face. I added this to the best man speech:

> *Sir Winston Churchill is quoted as saying, "My most brilliant achievement was my ability to be able to persuade my wife to marry me." Leo, congratulations on persuading Candice to marry you. I know from experience how much of a challenge it is to convince a girl to marry.*

I was recently rejected by an anonymous female, and I am relieved you don't have to suffer through the same disillusionment of a failed proposal. I know you will both be very happy for the first few years together; what happens after that, no one really knows. I suppose marriage is comparable to a puppy. It's adorable and full of life, but no one can predict whether or not it will get run over by a truck. Leo and Candice, perhaps you should keep each other on a tight leash. Now, let us raise our glasses to Leo and Candice. I want to propose a toast to the bride and groom. For the Spanish speakers, I want to propose "una tostada." May you find happiness together before, during, and after marriage, and may love never destroy you. Gracias.

The speech was finally complete. I looked out at all the buildings and trees as the sun began to set. It cast a beautiful orange hue on all the land. I must admit, the Argentine sun is far more glorious than ours. I understand why their flag has a sun on it. I leaned back in my wheelchair in admiration; Upon crossing my arms, I realized I had been severely burned by the sun. The whole family rushed to the French doors when they heard me scream. I was at a low. I told them I screamed out of pre-wedding jitters; no one believed me.

Candice and my mom went to the pharmacy to buy aloe vera. My dad, Leo Martinez, and my ex-lover remained with me. We sat in Leo's living room watching a rugby match on mute. Leo and my father occasionally nodded awkwardly at one another but didn't speak much. Lana and I pretended to watch rugby as a way to avoid making eye contact; it was a tribulation of sorts. I don't much care for United Statesian football, either, but at least they bring the game to a halt every fifteen seconds. Rugby is football without timeouts or commercials.

I asked Leo if he had any milk. To my disappointment, he brought me a cup of milk without a bag.

"Where's the bag?" I asked. He explained that no one drinks from the bag; I insisted that I did. He hesitantly brought me the entire milk bag.

I had lost all etiquette that day. My skin was blistered, my back was broken, and my heart was pummeled. I chugged the rich milk directly from the bag. Like a baby eyeing its surroundings while drinking a bottle, my eyes panned back and forth across the room. No one said a word, but I could see their judging eyes. I glanced at Lana and saw that she was staring at a drop of milk cascading down my chin. She put her head down to avoid looking at me. I really didn't care what she thought at the time.

One thing the doctor failed to explain about my pain medication is that it made my stomach weaker. He also failed to explain that, when in a wheelchair, it is difficult to act fast in urgent situations. Suddenly, as I made direct eye contact with Lana, a half-gallon of rich milk made a round trip back from my stomach. I was drenched in the essence of organic Argentine produce. Candice and my mother returned at that inopportune moment.

"What happened!?" exclaimed Candice. No one else spoke; the situation spoke for itself. Lana and I were now avoiding eye contact with each other even more than before.

The next morning, we arose early, got dressed, and made our way to the van for the wedding ceremony. It was nearly impossible fitting into my suit with the back brace. I looked like an undercover cop with a bulletproof vest bulging under my tuxedo. I was on crutches for the day as my legs still felt tingly. I was slightly concerned one of the mafia members would attempt to stab me. We arrived at the cathedral where a crowd gathered outside. The wedding planner had decided it would be a good idea to have a guest list at the door.

As we stood in line, I felt extremely vulnerable to any attacks, emotional or otherwise. Lana attempted to hold my hand, but I crutched away from her. I was ignoring her as a subtle way to help her feel the pain she had caused me. I've learned through studies of the ancient Amish that shunning can be an extremely painful experience to the shunee. After Lana had rejected my proposal, I had set the long-term goal for myself to get Lana to marry me; ignoring her was only the first step of many.

The wedding went horribly. I found, through personal experience, that throwing uncooked rice at a bride is only acceptable after the ceremony. A grain of rice became momentarily lodged in the corner of Candice's eye, delaying the proceedings by five minutes. My pain medication was also starting to wear off, causing me to feel excruciating pain in my back. As the ceremony went on, my mother wept with a smile as my father sued his eyes for welling with tears. I wondered why they weren't happier about their first-born daughter getting married.

The reception wasn't much better. Right at the moment the best man was supposed to read the speech, fat Voltaire imposed, giving an impromptu groomsman speech. By the time he was done, there was no time for my speech. I was outraged at his inconsideration, but I didn't want to cause a scene. To contain my rage, I bit my tongue, quite literally, and cut much deeper than I had intended. I could taste the minerals in my blood; from the taste, I deduced I was slightly deficient in iron. I soaked up the blood with the paper I had written my speech on. It was poetic of me.

At the reception, I did get to take my next dose of pain meds. I also drank a glass of champagne. The two mixed in my system and caused me to feel mildly unstable, both emotionally and physically.

Across the yard, I spotted Lana dancing with one of Leo's cousins; it struck a nerve in me. I knew my spine was fractured and dancing would have been agonizing for me, but watching her dance with him was somehow more painful. I hobbled over to Lana. My proceeding regrettable action resulted in the breakup of a beautiful couple. It is the fourth worst thing I've done to sabotage a romantic relationship. It's also the worst thing I've done to Lana. In my defense, I must list several actions that I did NOT engage in that would have been far worse than what I actually did.

I DID NOT:

1. Kiss another girl to make Lana jealous.

2. Get drunk and insult Lana through a microphone.

3. Have sex with another girl.

4. Throw cake at Lana.

5. Flash anyone (except in the restroom accidentally)

6. Physically harm Lana or anyone else.

7. Publicly defecate.

With those possibilities out of the way, I will now explain what I actually did.

"Oh, let me see that necklace for a sec," I said to Lana as casually as possible.

With curiosity, she handed me her silver necklace. Without hesitation, I balled the necklace up in my fist then hurled it into the man-made pond nearby. It only took me 2.483 seconds to regret my decision, but it was too late. Lana raised her hand to slap me but restrained herself. At that moment she had one of those man cries. She stared into my eyes ferociously, unflinchingly, as a single teardrop rolled down her cheek.

"This is over, Jeremy," she said softly before walking away. I would have preferred the slap.

To help you to understand the full impact of the silver necklace, I need to backtrack a little. When Lana and I began dating, she had a gold necklace she wore everywhere; it was the same necklace I'd stolen after the car crash during driver's ed. If you recall, me returning it to her led to our first kiss in her driveway. The gold necklace belonged to her dead grandmother and meant the world to Lana.

One day Lana came to my house sobbing. Her dead grandmother's golden necklace had been stolen from the girls' locker room during a gym class. It was the first time I saw her cry. We sat on the swinging chair on my front porch until she ran out of tears.

The next day, we met up in the library. This is when I handed her a heart-shaped, rusty, silver pendant necklace.

"My grandma gave this to me when I was a baby," I told her. "She thought I was a girl. She was a super nice human, and she would have adopted you as her granddaughter anyway." This was the first time Lana told me she loved me. She wore that necklace every day from that moment on. That necklace, of course, is the same one I threw into the pond.

The worst part of the entire trip was the twelve-hour return flight home. Lana and I sat next to each other heartbroken and speechless for the entire duration of the flight. The pressurized cabin made my back hurt tormentingly. The oxycodone pills helped with my back pain as well as my heart pain. I purposely dropped a pill onto Lana's lap to help her get through the pain she was feeling; I pretended not to notice it drop. She subtly bit off half the pill and placed the other half in her pocket. Within a few minutes, we both managed to give each other a warm smile for closure. There's a quote that states, "All's well that ends well." It's a load of bullshit.

CHAPTER 7:
HOW TO COLLEGE

"If only a parrot could use a pencil, it would do exceedingly well in college."
-Jeremy Jude

I never went to college. It would be like Bill Gates taking computer lessons. Still, I loved academia and wanted to be surrounded by it. When I graduated high school, despite my mother's grave concerns about me living out on my own, my lawyer dad got me a job at a college on the western coast of these United States. My lawyer dad convinced her it was for the best. Lana had decided to attend an East Coast school, so I chose the opposite side of the country in order to be as far away from her as possible without leaving the comforts of a first world country. It had been two years since we broke up, but I, having flawless memory, thought of her every day. At one point during my junior year of high school, we saw each other at a Walmart. I pretended to watch one of the display TVs. My tactic would have worked better if we hadn't been standing in the fruit aisle. She caught me laughing at a pile of bananas.

I worked in the office of administration as an assistant. The college was a hole-in-the-wall campus nicknamed USC. I worked part-time, though I often had full-time hours on my schedule. I was also busy teaching several graduate level courses pro bono. In the evenings, I would often find a party to attend. It was not for my entertainment; I was simply there to observe. I've attended over fifty-six college parties altogether and have developed some impressive theories about the cultural practice based on my observations.

I found beer pong strangely primitive. The objective of the game was to see how filthy one could get a ping pong ball before throwing it into an opponent's beverage. I used to play a similar game in middle school, only my opponents were bullies, and I used my father's prescription laxative pills instead of ping pong balls.

I attempted to befriend a household of fraternity brothers; interestingly enough, none of them were actually biologically related. They were rather friendly and civil, but I quickly found that we lacked any common interests. They were obsessed with the size and shape of one another's reproductive organs. My cue to leave was when they pulled down their trousers and began visual comparisons. I asked a sorority sister if women did the same thing in their cult.

"Uh...we're not a cult," she said with reproach; I laughed in her cultish face.

One of the perks of working in the administrative office was free housing. They gave me a room in one of the co-ed dorms. Of course, these were the cheapest dorms intended for freshmen and persons belonging to the lower class. My dad offered to pay for me to be in the nice dorms, but I felt immoral taking his lawyer blood money. It was bad enough that he had helped me get the job in the first place. Still, it would have been nice to have my own bathroom. On the up side, my room had a sink, and my brilliant mind learned to survive with what I had.

Across the hall from me lived a curious redheaded girl named Bethany. She had a subtle nose piercing, startling blue eyes, and excellent facial bone structure. She was annoyingly free-spirited and would always invite me places with her group of friends. We had opposite tastes in everything from music to movies. Every time I told her about one of my ingenious theories, she would laugh uncontrollably and compliment my "dry sense of humor." If soul mates existed, Bethany and I were soul antagonists. Still, we somehow became friends.

One college incident that especially stands out was when I was kicked out of the biochemical engineering class I was teaching. This wasn't the first time it had happened. I was at my wits' end with the college—I was teaching several of these courses at no charge to them, yet they continuously dis-appreciated the level of intellect I was adding to their corporation. My students laughed as campus security escorted me off the premises. I waited an hour before returning to my dorm.

The next day, I stormed into the office of a one President Morian (pronounced "Moron"). "Mister Moron, I'm resigning as professor. Take me off the rooster." I demanded.

"The rooster?" He asked, attempting to play dumb with me. I pulled out a crumpled paper from my pocket and dropped it on his desk.

"I won't be needing this any more!" I said. Mr. Moron unwrinkled the paper with a confused frown.

Once he read the contents, he yelled, "Where the hell did you get my diploma!?" I pointed to an empty picture frame on his wall.

"You're not very observant, are you?" I said. I had lifted it three weeks prior, when I was brought into his office for "impersonating a professor." Again, I was unnecessarily escorted off campus by security. I was fortunate the college was so large; they never realized I worked and lived on campus.

I returned to my dorm and threw my books out the window. Unfortunately, I am excellent at cleaning windows. By the time I realized the window was closed, my books had hit the ground outside. There was a knock at my door. It was Bethany wondering what had happened. When she saw the shattered window, she laughed.

"What the freak did you do, man?" she asked with an irritating giggle. I stared at her blankly, which only made her laugh more. I told her I was in no mood for her free-spirited laughter and asked her to leave me be.

Fifteen minutes later, we were on a bus. Bethany had somehow convinced me it would cheer me up.

"This was a terrible idea, Bethy," I muttered under my pessimistic breath. I often called her Bethy, and at times Bethy Lethy; I only added the "Lethy" when I was in a great mood. She often called me Jer Bear. I once asked her to refer to me as J-Dog; she laughed in my face, and we never spoke of it again.

Bethany pulled out her MP3 player and offered to share an earbud with me.

"Next," I commanded, as the first song sounded more like clamor and screeching than music. By the fifteenth "next" in a row, I gave up on listening to her music.

"Where are we going?" I asked.

"We goin' to San Francisco, yo!" she said obnoxiously. This was not how she actually spoke, but she used this sort of language in a joking manner frequently. She knew it annoyed me. There is a term used to describe people that care deeply about proper grammar and English: a "grammar Nazi." As a genius, I am a grammar führer. I asked her to speak as she normally does.

"My B, dawg, my B." She said jokingly, fully aware of its irritating effect. I turned my head away. She laughed to herself.

In San Francisco, we ate at a seafood restaurant by the ocean. The waiter asked us what we were celebrating.

"What makes you think we're celebrating?" I asked. He thought we were a couple. I told him we were a couple of friends. He apologized and removed our dirty plates.

"This is nice," said Bethany.

"I have to pee," said I.

I went to the restroom and upon my return found another man in my seat. He was smiling and asking Bethany many questions. I approached this reproachable gentleman and asked him why he was in my seat.

"Oh my gosh, dude, are you together? I'm so sorry!" he said manipulatively.

"Yes," I replied. "We are a couple and we're celebrating our tenth anniversary." It was certainly too high a number, but I corrected the mistake by adding: "It's amazing that even as little eight-year-olds we knew we were soul mates." To seal the deal I went in for a kiss, but he jumped out of my seat before I could plant one on him. Had he been bisexual, my plan would have backfired. Bethy laughed uncontrollably as she exclaimed, "Dude, I can't believe you freaking attempted to kiss another dude!" She was unaware it wasn't my first time using this tactic.

After lunch, we decided to go to a strip mall. I was disappointed to see everyone fully clothed. As it turns out, a strip mall is just a mall without a roof. Bethany wanted to enter every store; I wanted to enter none. We spent two hours looking through stores and bought nothing. On our way to the bus stop, Bethany spotted a tattoo shop called Black and Blue. She had no tattoos but had talked about getting one every day since I met her. She entered the parlor, and I reluctantly followed. I asked why she planned on getting a lifelong tattoo as impulsively as one would buy a donut.

"I dunno. What should I get?" she asked me. I suggested she get something that would still be relevant decades later, like her social security number. She chose a tattoo of a couple purple triangles on her rib cage. It was uneventful.

I devoted much of my time at the college to finding a new soul mate to replace Lana. Bethany eventually stopped bringing her friends around, as the routine habit I had developed was to question these girls' intelligence. My intention was not to make anyone feel small or belittled; I was only looking for intellectual compatibility. Still, the primary response of these girls was to take offense. The end result was usually a low-self-esteem-induced date. These dates never ended well. I once took a girl to play mini golf, and we ended up furiously competing, which was fun. The date went south when I defeated her and she began sobbing her eyes out.

"I hate my dad so much!" she exclaimed tearfully. Apparently, I reminded her of her competitive father, which was no surprise to me; I've always been a very paternal figure among women. I brought her a cup of water and gave her a hug. One thing led to another, and we ended up French kissing for an hour in her car. I felt nothing for her.

One day, I complained to Bethany about all my failed dates. She told me to stop trying to deny my feelings for the girl I still clearly loved.

"Bethany, I love you as a friend," I said, clarifying. She sighed loudly and said, "You're such an idiot!" To be fair, I never told her I was a savant; savantism and idiocy, I've found, are often confused.

As my desperation to be in a relationship with a female increased, I noticed the amount of attractive women around me skyrocket. When I was with Lana, I would see an average of 3.2 attractive women per week. After we broke up, every girl I interacted with was attractive. My gifted brain emanated sensuality on a subconscious level in a way that lured attractive females to me; this was beneficial considering my conscious self was uninterested in flirting.

I have found, through a process of trial and error, that confidence is important when attracting a mate. I've always had a glut of confidence and a superfluity of charm, but I had been keenly unaware of their positive effects on women. Initially, I attempted to enchant them with far-fetched tales of being cripplingly insecure. When that failed, I pretended to have low self-esteem. Perhaps the most ineffective experiment I tried was to pretend to be so shy I could not muster up the courage to speak.

I stumbled upon my discovery of confidence being significant almost accidentally, as all great discoveries are made. Bethy and I were sitting together at an Olive Garden; it wasn't a date. I was in a terrible mood; not even the five packets of sugar in my water lifted my spirits. Bethany was telling me yet another story of how a guy attempted to get her phone number. I said nothing.

"What's up? Are you in a bad mood or something?" she asked calmly.

"I'm just tired of waiting for my steak fajitas." I lied.

"You ordered ravioli," she said, calling my bluff.

Just then, our waitress approached with our food. I had attempted to flirt with her before we ordered. I had told her my mother neglected me, and that as a result I was constantly trying to fill that void with hotties like her. My flirtations were not as effective as I had hoped. As the waitress set our food down she asked, "Can I get you guys anything else?" Something came over me; it was a mix of irritability and hunger. I looked at Bethany and said, "Fuck it." She had no idea what I was talking about.

I looked this waitress in the eyes and said, "You're absolutely gorgeous and I find it intolerable that I don't know how to ask you on a date." The waitress was flustered.

"I thought you were a couple," she said shyly. I explained to her that Bethy was my wing girl but had been doing an awful job setting me up with girls. In the end, I took this beautiful waitress out to eat at a different Olive Garden. She never called me back.

I'll end this chapter in my life and in my book here because my college years were relatively repetitive. Bethany and I went on adventures, I went on meaningless dates with girls, and eventually I resigned from my job in the administration office when they attempted to fire me for "impersonating the Dean." I was flattered by their assumption, but my impersonation of James Dean doesn't do him justice.

I suppose it's noteworthy to mention that Bethany and I did get engaged for a year; It was one of those desperate decisions spurred out of curiosity and licentious desires. We called off the wedding when we attempted to create a music playlist for the reception. I wanted Chopin; She wanted a rapper named Fifteen Scents. Music wasn't our downfall; it was just a signpost guiding us to acknowledge how wrong we were for each other.

My three years spent on college property taught me several invaluable lessons about life, five of which I have included for my readers' learning benefit:

- "College student" is not synonymous with "educated person."

- Redheaded, free-spirited girls can make surprisingly good friends.

- Borrowing a college president's diploma has negative consequences, even if you return it.

- Soul mates are unbelievably hard to find and not easily replaced by flings.

- After college, most humans feel just as lost as they did before college. (Note that I am not referring to myself; I, being a genius, found myself while there.)

CHAPTER 8:
TWENTY-ONE

"I can stop gambling whenever I want to; it just so happens
that I never want to stop."
-Jeremy Jude

After resigning from my position at the college and leaving Bethy behind, I returned to my hometown and paid a visit to my parents' house. I was now twenty-one years old. Upon entering the house, I was attacked by a proud mother, specifically mine.

"My baby boy is a college graduate!" she exclaimed as she squeezed the life out of me. My dad shook my hand.

"Well done," he said.

"No, medium rare," I replied with a chuckle. He was confused. My dad is notoriously awful at joking.

"We'll have to throw you a big graduation party!" exclaimed my mother.

Convincing my parents I was attending college all those years was neither easy nor difficult; it was simply necessary. I used the university account of a student named Geoffrey Willard to have my dad transfer tuition money. I gave Geoffrey five percent of my earnings, and in exchange, he gave me access to his unofficial transcripts each semester. A graphic design student modified the transcripts to have my name on them. I'd simply send the transcripts to my father at the end of each semester.

"You need to raise your GPA this semester," he'd say, at which point I'd pay Geoffrey an additional five percent to study harder. When I "graduated," I had the graphic design student modify Geoffrey's diploma to have my name on it. I thought I would be exposed when my mother had at first suggested flying out to California to attend my graduation; fortunately, my mom was too busy with a hernia, and my dad was too busy lawyering.

At my graduation party, I received a grand total of $7,632.21; my lawyer dad naturally had wealthy lawyer friends. To my surprise and perturbation, Lana also made an appearance at my graduation party. My misguided mother, whom I love dearly, thought it would be nice for us to see each other again. I thought it best to avoid Lana. About halfway through the party, I saw her starting to approach me and attempted to hide behind a houseplant in order to avoid her. It didn't work. She asked me how I was doing; I asked her the same.

We spoke for a while, and I managed to carry on with the traditional small talk that happens between two former lovers, until I heard the words "my boyfriend" come from her mouth (not in reference to me). I opened my mouth to speak, but no words came out. I'm not much of a crier—I've only cried 463 times in my life— but I had the strangest, strongest, most startling urge to cry. I didn't even cry when Bethany and I called off the wedding. But then, Lana had always affected me in a way that no one else ever had.

"Please excuse me, Lana," I finally said with synthetic composure. I walked out of the house to the front yard where people were mingling and laughing. Distraught, I furiously flung my graduation cap in the air. Everyone around me cheered at my misery, and it suddenly seemed that I did not belong here. The rest of the party dragged by slowly, and Lana didn't try to talk to me again.

That night, I purchased a one-way ticket to Las Vegas, Nevada. The next morning I realized my decision may have been a little too impulsive, so I changed the ticket to round trip. I planned on taking my graduation money and "gambling" it all. I put "gambling" in quotation marks because it's not really gambling if your brain is a human calculator; it's more like stealing from the casino. No one steals from the casinos, except for humans with gifted minds.

I arrived in Las Vegas like an Italian immigrant arriving at Ellis Island. Upon exiting the airport, I was hit with an unnatural amount of heat.

"Is this heat safe?" I asked a security guard.

"Supposed to be 115 degrees today," he replied, as though that was a normal temperature to declare. I hated him.

I hailed a taxi and ordered the driver to take me to Caesar's Palace. I chose Caesar's Palace as my gambling destination due to its rich historical background. The city of Las Vegas wasn't even built until 1905, meaning Julius Caesar built his palace in the desert centuries before anyone else lived there. Perhaps it was his vacation palace.

I walked into the historical fortress like a multimillionaire in disguise. Most humans assume multimillionaires are easily recognizable; most multimillionaires actually wear worn-down jeans with sandals. Think of Steve Jobs or Spock Zuckerberg. I marveled at the statues of Caesar everywhere, standing tall and majestic like they had been for millennia. I asked the front desk attendant how old the building was. She said it was built in 1966.

"BC?" I asked.

"AD," she replied with a cheesy grin. She was clearly an idiot.

I decided to book a deluxe room for the week. At three hundred dollars a night, it was quite a bargain. After all, I was there to become an overnight millionaire; lodging expenses were champ change to me. (I prefer "champ change" to "chump change" because it makes those with chump change feel good about themselves.) I made my way down to the casino. A cock-tailed waitress offered me a free beverage.

"Nice try," I stated boldly. I knew casinos were almost as greedy as lawyers; why would this one ever offer anything free without motive? I deduced the beverages were laced with judgment-inhibiting drugs.

I found the blackjack table where the players had the most beverages; this already gave me an edge over my drugged-up competitors.

"The minimum bet is fifty dollars, sir," said the dealer of cards.

"Make it a cool five hundred dollars," I said unflinchingly. My competitors were impressed, but they still matched my bet.

The objective of blackjack is to get as close to 21 points as possible using the card values without going over 21. The player who's closest to 21 gets all the money. The dealer plays as well, which isn't fair considering he practices every day. It's a game of luck to most, but an elite few are able to count cards and win based on skill alone. Counting cards is when one keeps track of all the cards on the table; When the sum of all the cards reaches 13 it is extremely likely the next card drawn will get you very close to 21. It's a sure thing. Unfortunately, only geniuses can successfully count cards; fortunately, I am a genius.

The dealer dealt out five cards, one of which was for him. I drew a 9.

"Hit me," said one of the competitors to the dealer. The dealer kept calm and handed the man another card instead.

"Hit me," said the next competitor. I was surprised by the culture of aggression blackjack seemed to possess. The dealer didn't react; instead, he dealt yet another card. I watched in disgust as each successive player took his turn and told this poor dealer to hit him. When the dealer got to me, I said, "Don't hit me; just give me another card, please."

He confirmed my answer and handed me another card. It was an 11, leaving me with a total of 20 points. I had only one point to go. I counted all the cards on the table; there were ten cards total. If it reached 13, I was golden.

"Hit me," said the first competitor again. I was sure the dealer would tear the man's head off, but again, he just gave him a card to deescalate the situation.

"Stand," commanded the next competitor to the dealer.

"He is standing, you goose!" I exclaimed rather aggressively. I detest bullying in all contexts.

This time the dealer stood up for himself and refused to give this coward another card. The next competitor said "hit me" again to the dealer, and I nearly lost it.

"I'll hit you if you want," I said in a calm voice, though my jaw was clenched. The dealer handed the man another card.

"You need to stand up for yourself, bud," I said softly to the dealer. When the next competitor said "stand," I stared at the dealer and nodded firmly. The dealer refused to give the competitor another card.

"I'm very proud of you," I said to the dealer. I became so caught up in all the drama that I had forgotten to count the cards. I quickly scanned the table and counted only twelve cards; I needed thirteen cards on the table to be guaranteed a 21. It was looking bleak. I considered using one last trick I had up my sleeve; it was a deck of cards, but the deck wasn't the same color or design as the casino cards, so I just kept it tucked away. I frowned at the dealer and said, "It's just not in the cards for me today." He asked if I wanted another card.

"It won't do any good, bud. Trust me on this," I said remorsefully. To this day, I don't know how he got away with it, but he somehow made it seem like my 20 beat everyone else's scores. He handed me my winnings. I stood to my feet and went in to shake his hand.

"Sir, you're not allowed to make contact with me," he said. He was being a little extreme, but that's part of the process when someone learns to stand up for themselves.

I was five hundred dollars richer, but it took me over five minutes to earn this much. At this rate, I calculated that it would have taken me approximately...

$$12 \times \$500 = \$6000 \text{ per hour}$$

166 hours just to make my first million. That meant that it would take me roughly...

6.75 days. I apologize to my readers for the extravagant and unintentionally flaunty mathematical equations left on these pages. I do not mean for them to be an arrogant display of my ingenious mind, but rather, a humble explanation of my calculations.

I made my way to the casino's cashier window.

"Could I have 7,632 one-dollar chips, please?" I asked the stewardess at the window. She counter-offered with $100 chips instead.

"I tell you what, let's do five-dollar chips," I said exactly as James Bond would have (The Pierce Brosnan Bond, not Sean Connery). I was low-balling her, and she didn't even know it.

"Sir, that's a lot of chips. Would you be okay with fifty-dollar chips instead?" she said compromisingly.

"Sold!" I said with a cheeky grin; I had played her like a violin. They loaded the chips into the bag and handed it to me. In the bag there were...

$$
\begin{array}{r}
152.64 \\
50\overline{)7632.00} \\
50 \\
\hline
263 \\
250 \\
\hline
0132 \\
100 \\
\hline
320 \\
300 \\
\hline
200
\end{array}
$$

exactly 152.64 chips. At 11.5 grams each, I was carrying a bag weighing...

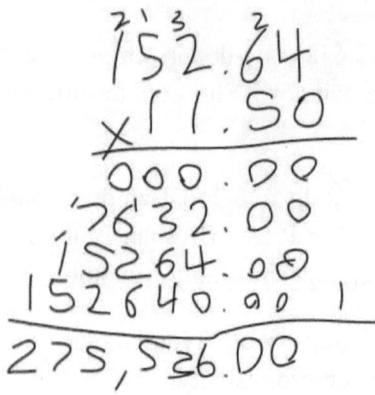

275,536.00 grams. In American pounds, that's roughly...

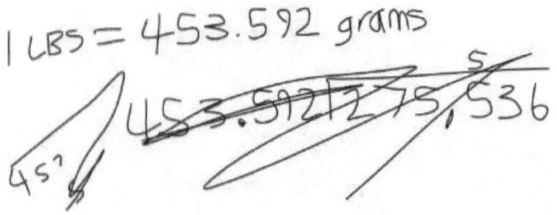

a lot of pounds. The exact amount is irrelevant to this story. I began walking towards the crap table, which was not exactly what I thought it was. Crap, as it turns out, is a casino game. My plan for playing crap was to allow the subconscious part of my mind to tell me when to place my bet; then I was going to go "all in." ("All in" is a casino term used when one goes "all in" on a gamble.) I approached the crap game and dumped my 152.64 chips all over the table to assert my dominance.

"All in!" I exclaimed.

"Sir, you need to get larger chips. These are too many!" said the crap dealer nervously. Just then I felt a tap on my shoulder and heard a female voice from behind me say, "Excuse me, sir, is your name Jeremy Jude?"

She was a casino employee, so I wasn't sure I could trust her. She may have been trying to incriminate me for counting cards.

"Jeremy actually went to the police station to greet his old friend, the chief of the Las Vegas Police Department," I cleverly answered. "Why do you ask?"

"Your sister is on the phone for you. She said it was urgent." The woman had wide eyes and seemed sincere. I decided to remain calm just in case this was a ploy to entrap me. The task of filling my empty bag with 152.64 chips seemed daunting. I began picking them up one by one, then calmly asked the crap dealer and the phone lady to collect them with me. It only took us 34.751 seconds to fill the bag.

They handed me a phone at the front desk lobby of Caesar's Palace.

"Hello?" I asked into the phone, though I already knew it was Candice. I still remember the exact phrasing she used. Of course, I remember all words everyone has ever said to me, but this remembrance is far more detailed. "Mom was in a bad accident," she said, "It's serious." Her voice trembled and cracked; She spoke as one would walk through a field full of landmines, aware that at any moment she could erupt into waterworks.

I asked her if my mother would live, to which Candice replied, "You need to come home, okay?" My body reacted strangely to these words; muscle tension and increased heart rate were the symptoms. It was as though my muscles knew something I didn't. They were commanding me to leave at once. I've learned to trust my body; the last time I ignored its signs I ended up owning my neighbor a new carpet.

I sprinted out of Caesar's Palace with my bag of casino chips and hailed a cab to the airport. By the time I realized I had left my suitcase at the hotel, we had already arrived at the airport.

"Your total's gonna be fifteen dollars and thirty-two cents," said the cabby. I handed him a fifty-dollar chip and asked if he had change.

"I can't accept these," he said sternly. I mulled over my options and decided on a rational solution; I took off in a full sprint as I yelled to the cabby, "Yo home, smell ya later!" To be honest, I learned that clever line from an actor named William Smith.

The flight home was grueling, as all flights tend to be. My least favorite moment was when an elderly woman attempted to grab her orthopedic pillow from the overhead bin and caused my bag of chips to fall and spill out over the aisle. I left that flight with only 137.64 casino chips; undoubtedly, pillow lady pocketed a few when I wasn't looking.

Leo Martinez was the one who picked me up from the airport. In spite of the grave circumstances, I was filled with joy to see the godlike lion. He drove us to the hospital, where Candice and my lawyer dad were waiting in the lobby.

"Hey, bud, how was your flight?" said Candice in that whispering-to-avoid-crying tone. She gave me a gentle hug. My dad stood up and patted me on the shoulder like a robot imitating human emotion. His eyes were bloodshot; he was either high, or he had been crying, but neither of those causes seemed likely.

"How's Mom?" I asked.

"She's in surgery right now so they won't really know until she's stable," my dad replied. He had a demeanor I'd never seen on him before; it was human weakness.

"How are you doing?" I asked him. I was more curious than concerned. At that moment, he began to sob uncontrollably in front of us. I've never felt closer to my dad than at that moment of pure, uninhibited, human vulnerability. I saw my lawyer dad as I had never seen him and would never see him again – as a person with limitations and flaws instead of a lawyer steeped in rhetoric and stoicism. I deduced from this, however, that my mother was in dire condition. Seeing my father cry made it all too real for me.

I realize this chapter is growing dark, but my tendency as a genius is to be objective about life. I have no desire to cotton candy-coat my stories, nor can I in good conscience do so. It is only through the darkest chapters of one's experience that true life can be reached. In the end, things turned out okay for my mother, and the funeral was lovely.

I do apologize for the insensitive nature of that last joke. I feel obliged to tell you my mother is alive and well, though I'm getting ahead of myself.

We sat in the lobby for hours, waiting for any update whatsoever regarding my mother. During that time, I tasted half the items in the vending machine, made a pyramid of casino chips, drew a Charlie Chaplin mustache on all the faces in the magazines, and rearranged some of the furniture. There was nothing left to do but sit and wait. We were all miserable.

Late into the evening, Lana's parents visited the hospital and brought us food from a restaurant, but none of us could eat. I certainly didn't have an appetite, partly because I was filled with vending machine treats. They sat in the lobby with us and assured us they weren't going anywhere.

"Is that a threat?" I said jokingly, which startled them for a moment. I should not have yelled it.

Lana's parents genuinely liked me; I deduced that Lana had never told them what I had done at my sister's wedding. My casino chip pyramid sparked a conversation between us, and we talked for quite a while until eventually they asked if I was dating anyone. I told them I wasn't. I had heard from my parents that Lana had been dating a jock on the debate team at her college. I subtly asked how Lana's boyfriend was.

"Oh, they only dated for two months. She broke it off with him a few weeks ago," said Mr. Allen with a casual wave of his hand. "Don't tell her I told you." He added as he winked at me.

"What has Lana been doing the past three years?" I asked.

"Studying. She's double majoring in art history and economics," explained Mrs. Allen.

"Just studying?" I asked.

"Well, she's had a very full schedule. Oh, there she is!" said Mrs. Allen as Lana walked through the door.

I watched Lana embrace my sister, then my father, then Leo, until she made her way over to me.

"Can I sit here?" she asked, as though I were a stranger at a bus stop. I did not get a hug. I nodded, and she sat next to me. She looked beautiful, as she always had, which annoyed me.

I was further annoyed by her continued mysterious effect on both my mind and body. My mother was dying, yet I found myself distracted and morphed by Lana's presence. I was beginning to feel guilty about focusing on Lana while my mother's life was in the balance, until Lana asked me how my mom was and brought me back to my reason for being in the hospital. My response was one of those attempts to start a sentence that inevitably failed due to strong emotion. As I've said before, I'm not a crier; Lana just had a very disarming aura about her.

Lana embraced me as masculine tears rolled off my cheeks onto the horribly outdated hospital tile. I rarely cry, but when I do, I cry a manly, silent cry in which the face remains undistorted but tears just fall stealthily. She rubbed my back gently for what seemed like hours. There was a quality about her that could end wars. It was a quality that surpassed the influence of even the most brilliant men. Admittedly, her power nearly surpasses my influence as a savant.

The next morning, I awoke to the sound of an announcement over the PA system system. My head rested on Lana's shoulder, wet from my drool. Within the hour, a nurse's assistant escorted us to the room where my mother was placed. My mother looked awful; a full body cast was not a good look on her. We sat around her bed and chit-chatted for a while until she fell asleep from boredom. I invited Lana to go to breakfast with me.

"I don't know if that's a good idea," she said quite persuasively. As I've stated before, I always take an "I don't know" to mean "Convince me, please!"

CHAPTER 9:
BREAKFAST AT TIMOTHY'S

"A wise man knows when and how to quit, but never does."

—Jeremy Jude

I took Lana to an old diner called Timothy's Hotcakes. The food was notoriously terrible, but the restaurant was near the hospital.

"How are your waffles?" I asked Lana.

"They're actually not very good," she replied. I assured her that was to be expected. There was a lull in the conversation after that. The only rational action during lulls is to say or do the first thing that comes to mind, no matter how vapid or witless.

I picked up two tiny coffee creamers—the plastic ones that resemble thimbles—and said, "Lana, have you ever seen those powerlifters that explode soda cans with their bare hands?" I pretended to squeeze the creamers as a powerlifter would; I didn't know my own strength. Both creamers exploded onto Lana's face. I was convinced this wouldn't help my chances of winning her back and wondered if the tinge of discomfort I felt could have been embarrassment; it wasn't. We sat in silence for a moment. The sight of cream dripping down Lana's innocent face was terrifying.

"These creamers must be on recall," I said. She began to chuckle, and that chuckle escalated to a full belly laugh (not that I was staring at her belly). Tears rolled down her eyes as she cackled. I worried the food had affected her brain. As it turns out, she simply thought the situation was humorous.

We talked for hours. She shared her experiences over the past years, which included a few stories of her ex-boyfriends; I hated those stories. She told a couple of stories, too, that she said had made her think of me. Those were my favorite stories. Eventually, I shared the story of Bethany and my engagement. Lana was surprised to hear of it.

Our conversation got a little more serious as we began to discuss our breakup at my sister's wedding in Argentina. I listened as Lana explained how my actions on that day hurt her deeply. I created a list of excuses in my brain, but I deduced that Lana was somehow fully in the right. As objective as I am, I could not have used those excuses. Instead, I apologized.

"Thanks. I forgive you," said Lana in a tone that conveyed she forgave me but no longer trusted me. I knew that tone from my childhood dentist, whose finger I'd almost bitten off. He said "I forgive you" and dropped me as a client the next day.

"It was nice catching up with you, Lana," I said calmly as we stood to exit. Lana asked why I was tearing up; I wiped my eyes discreetly as we headed out the door.

"Keep me posted on your mom, okay?" She patted me on the shoulder then walked to her car. I knew that the next time we saw each other it would be in a friend zone, like Pizza Hut's afternoon buffet.

I jogged over to Lana.

"Hey, I have something of yours!" I hollered. I had waited until the last minute to return it to her. She turned to see what it was, and I walked to meet her. I placed a very rusted, silver pendant necklace in her hand.

"You could probably get a solid twenty bucks for it at a pawn shop," I explained. She examined the necklace and looked at me with a wide-eyed, shocked expression.

"How do you have this?" she whispered.

"I went back to the pond," I explained. She stared at me for quite a while, and this time I could see tears welling up in her eyes.

"You went back to the pond? When?"

"When I visited Leo's parents last year."

"Your mom said you'd gone out there, but..." she shook her head as though witnessing a magician decapitating a bird.

"Was it hard to find?" she asked.

"No."

It had actually been quite treacherous. I spent four days searching for the necklace in murky waters. I eventually found it in the shallow end of the pond. "Sorry it took so long to return," I said.

"Are you sure you still want me to have it?"

"It's already yours," I explained. "I'm not a give-and-taker." (Full disclosure to my readers: I actually used the term "Indian giver" but I've recently found it is offensive to use, especially when saying it to a legitimate Native American chief; it's another story I won't get into, but he was being a real give-and-taker.)

Sensing our interaction was coming to an end, I gave Lana a hug and headed to my car. She approached me to ask if I'd be around. There was another lull in our talking, and I wanted to impress her, so I blurted out the first thing that came to mind.

"I'm actually heading to New York to become a fashion model." After speaking, I deduced I had two options to rectify my verbal misfire; I either had to tell her I was lying and apologize, or I had to move to New York. I chose the more rational of the solutions.

CHAPTER 10:
A NEW YORK MODEL

"I don't understand why being fashionably late is acceptable to society, but being fashionably absent is frowned upon."

—Jeremy Jude

"I beseech you!" I yelled to Leo at the breakfast table; Candice and Leo had invited me over for breakfast at their new home. They had just moved into town after Candice received her doctorate in chemistry.

"Calm down and tell us what you're talking about," said my sister, interrupting me. I rebutted, saying, "I love you, but you're a terrible listener." Leo clarified to me that we had been eating in complete silence when out of nowhere I had yelled, "I beseech you!" I leaned back in my chair and laughed.

"I guess you're right!" I said. Although some people may find it strange that I sometimes confuse thought with talk, this is actually a common occurrence among geniuses. This happens because our brains are large enough to touch the inner tubules of the ear canal. As a result, our thoughts are amplified to the point that it becomes difficult to distinguish thoughts from external speech.

"I beseech you," I repeated, looking back and forth at them, "to help me land a talent agent in New York!" This time I'd said it unquestionably out loud. Leo came from a multi-million dollar family, and who ever heard of a multimillionaire that didn't have contacts in every city of the world?

"I don't know any talent agents in New York," said Leo, lying through his perfectly symmetrical white teeth.

"Oh, maybe your dad would," said Candice. Leo took a huge bite of his pancake. The whole stuffing-your-face-to-delay-talking bit is always ineffective. Candice and I waited patiently for Leo to chew and swallow his food.

"I'm not sure it's a good idea," said Leo finally.

"Oh, come on, he could make it as a model," argued Candice. "He's a very attractive man." It was an odd sentence coming from my sister.

Leo ended up contacting his father to let him know about my request. His father knew many people in New York. Leo told me his dad "called in a favor," which resulted in me getting signed by an agency. I didn't ask questions, as Leo's dad was the great gambini of the Martinez family mafia. I hoped this "favor" didn't result in too many casualties.

It took me two months to book my first modeling gig in New York. I finally lost the ten pounds my agent asked me to lose. I had been starving myself, mostly because I ran out of money for food and refused to ask my dad for any more; I did, however, allow him to pay for rent to give him the illusion that he was still a part of my life. The gig I landed was for a runway show at some small local festival they called Fashion Week. My slow start was something I had predicted. I was pushing the boundaries of my either-or theory.

My either-or theory states that for every strength there is an equal or opposite weakness. For example, if you are tall you can play basketball, but you cannot be a horse jockey. If your strength is computer programming, your weakness is being suave. If your strength is honesty and integrity, your weakness is being a politician. No one is exempt from this either-or theory; if your strength is being a genius, your weakness is modeling (not because of appearance, mind you). Now you see the issue I was facing.

I walked into my personal dressing room. It was filled with dozens of other models. The show's director, Gerald Acart, entered the room full of hope and despair. He was a small man with large glasses and salt-and-pepper hair.

"Okay, two hours to showtime everyone! We need to hustle our bustles!" he exclaimed with flair and elegance. I enjoyed the eccentric way he spoke. He had a constant tremor in his hands, occasionally quenched by holding a lit cigarette between his fingers. His face was always theatrical when he thought he was being watched. I once caught a glimpse of him during a moment of presumed privacy, though, and I saw the profundity of a man coping with a demanding career. Or, perhaps, he was simply allowing his food to digest.

He came striding towards me as he asked, "Okay, where have your pants gone mister? The gold ones with the white polka dots." Our fitting was the day before; the gold pants he was referring to were the ones I forgot to return to the tailor after the fitting. The bottom line is, I spilled a pan full of nachos on them.

"I suppose you caught me with my pants down!" I joked. He didn't laugh.

It was fascinating to watch Acart slowly fall apart as he asked everyone in the room if they'd seen the gold pants. He stomped back and forth frantically, taking an aggressive puff of nicotine into his lungs every few seconds.

"Mr. Acart, we can't smoke—" began one of the coordinators, quickly interrupted by his backlash.

"I know, I know! Can we not stress about my bad habit for a titch!? We have an EMERGENCY!"

With each passing minute he grew louder and louder until completely losing his mind.

"Okay, everyone stops what they're doing NOW!" he shouted at the top of his lungs, and the room froze. He continued, "Okay, we are not doing anything else until we locate the gold pants with the white polka dots! Everyone is looking, yes?" The models, hairdressers, and stylists stopped everything to look for the pants. I pretended to search as well, aware of its futility.

Mickey, the tailor from the fitting, grabbed my arm as he whispered in my ear, "Let me borrow you for a sec." Mickey was a six-foot, eight-inch, pale Norwegian weighing no more than 180.38 pounds. He escorted me to a room filled with sewing machines, mannequins, and fabric. He rummaged through the piles of fabric as he anxiously uttered, "Acart will have my ass on a platter if we don't fix this. What size are you?" My answer was, "Large," which meant nothing to Mickey.

I stood pantsless as Mickey cut gold fabric to my approximate measurements. With time being of the essence, he used thin velcro strips instead of sewing thread to assemble the pants. Mickey jogged around me to get a final look.

"It's good! Go, go, go!" he exclaimed as he gently shoved me out the door. As we jogged back, he pleaded with me not to reveal the pants were held together with velcro.

Mickey and I jogged into the dressing room where Acart was chastising his personal assistant. Upon seeing us, Acart dramatically dropped his clipboard and stared at me as though I were his long-lost child.

"Okay, holy Madonna and all her cherubim!" he said tearfully as he staggered towards my gold pants. Mickey asked if they were satisfactory; Acart kissed him on the hand.

"Okay, people!" shouted Acart. "Fiasco avoided! Sorry for my little tantrum! You know I love each and every one of you!" This touching moment would not have happened had I not ruined the first pair of gold pants.

Energetic trance music played out on the runway. I was overcome with exuberance. Acart gave me the signal, and I stepped onto the catwalk boldly. I was shocked to see thousands of attendees in the audience at this local festival. Hundreds of camera flashes pierced my retinas. As I walked to the front of the catwalk, I deduced that being remembered by a crowd this large would likely lead to greater opportunities. I was one of many models wearing strange clothing, so my gold pants would not make the memorable impression I needed. My gifted mind offered me a brilliant idea, and I walked with it.

I stood at the front of the runway with a dead expression. (This zombie-like aloofness is part of being a model.) Reaching down, I grabbed hold of my gold pants and tore them off my body like a dancer at a strip club. The velcro made it seem almost intentional. The crowd cheered loudly as I threw my gold pants at them. I later found out the pants landed on a friend of Acart's named Angelina Jolie. I blew kisses at everyone and jogged off stage.

Acart grabbed me by the shirt collar and yelled, "Okay, it is crazy how much trouble you are now in!" I was dismissed by him on the spot.

A few days later he called me with changed tones; Due to my pants-throwing incident his show was the most discussed topic of fashion week. He begged me to be in his next show, which I declined for no particular reason.

Within a few weeks, my agent, Miss Ellie, called me into her office.

"You're so hot right now!" she said.

"Thanks, you look pretty good, too, for a forty-year-old." She took it as an insult as she was only thirty-five. We discussed all the offers on the table. There were eight feature films offering me cameos, five talk shows requesting me to come in for an interview, and multiple offers for me to model internationally. I leaned back in my chair confidently.

"Here's what's going to happen," I said. I'll model for a year, and then I'm going to retire permanently from the industry."

She scoffed loudly.

I did exactly what I said. I modeled for a year in Russia and Poland then retired. It just wasn't for me. I thought about making those arduous months into a chapter in my memoirs, but they were rather uninteresting times. They mainly consisted of standing in front of a camera fourteen hours a day followed by late night meals with Russian models and, on multiple occasions, Putin's wife. The nature of our relationship was strictly platonic. Even these women, though, in all their cold beauty and power, were not quite what I was looking for.

My year as a model turned out to be a complete success, but I was relieved I never had to do it again. I was ready to go home and see what Lana had been doing with her life. When I returned to my hometown, she was gone. I found out from her parents that she was spending a few years studying at a university in Italy. They also cited some nonsense about her visiting the Batican, which I'm assuming is the Italian Batcave. I could not comprehend her ill-timed compulsion to leave town when things between us were finally being sorted out.

I wrote her a handwritten letter asking why she left without telling me. I preferred it to emails as, on rare occasions, my parents' internet would cut out for two minutes. My letter went something like this:

> Dear Lana,
>
> *I feel strongly that we have strong feelings for one another. I miss you terribly. Why did you leave without telling me? What if you return and we start our lives*

together? Thanks. Looking forward to your reply. xoxoxo

—Jeremy Jude

A week later, I got a letter from her. This is verbatim what it said:

> *Dear Jeremy,*
>
> *I wrote you eight letters while you were in New York, and Russia, and Poland. I guess I got tired of waiting for you to reply. You left for a year, remember? Please don't try to tell me you were unreachable or didn't get my letters. You sent my mom a thank you note when she sent cookies. I think it's best we both move on with our lives. Please know I will always care about you deeply. I hope only the best for your life.*
>
> *Sincerely,*
>
> *Lana*

Her point was valid; I had received all her letters. I had gone through an odd time of being infatuated with multiple Russian and Polish female coworkers; in fairness, they were supermodels. There were three or so I nearly dated, but something inside me stopped me. A part of me felt justified ignoring Lana as a sort of retribution for her rejecting my wedding proposal years earlier. I did have the strangest notion in my head that she never deserved my retribution, but I disregarded this notion and instead wrote her this:

> *Dear Lana,*
>
> *I'm sorry about the letters. Remember when I proposed to you, and you rejected my proposal? Perhaps this makes us even? I am not saying I refused to read your letters as petty revenge; I'm simply observing that Mother*

Karma may be paying you a visit, no? I apologize for any aggression this letter seems to convey. I say all these things in hopes to win back your heart. You're an extremely beautiful human inside and out. I think we should definitely date again. Thoughts? xoxoxo

-Jeremy Jude

She replied one last time. This letter came with a package. Her response utterly shattered me to my core:

Dear Jeremy,

You were the first boy I ever loved. When I was sixteen, I genuinely saw us lasting. I broke up with you because of a selfish act on your behalf. I'm aware you have since apologized, for which I am thankful, but this incident was one of many. Frankly, I don't see us getting back together. You've always been the kind of person to do exactly what is on your mind. While this quality has its benefits, it also makes you lack empathy towards anyone but yourself. Yes, there was something special between us, but a relationship is about two people, not one. If we dated, I would constantly worry about you suddenly deciding to move to China or buy a restaurant or something else equally as impulsive. I deserve better than you.

I'm returning your grandmother's silver necklace to you because it no longer seems appropriate for me to hold onto it. It should stay in your family as an heirloom.

As I've written before, we both need to move on with our lives. Please don't write me again.

Sincerely,

Lana

CHAPTER 11: THE UNENLIGHTENING

"Some drugs are to die for."

—Jeremy Jude

I sat on my parents' porch staring at Lana's letter for hours, gripping the silver necklace in my hand as if holding on to it could help me hold on to Lana. I contemplated the letter's many possible meanings. Could it be that Lana was attempting to forget about me completely?

Over the next two weeks, I felt like an entirely different person; I felt like a soldier recovering from war. I dreamt of Lana every night, and in the mornings I felt a dull pain in my chest. I stopped aiming when I peed, but even stranger, food tasted like cardboard. Apathy for all things weighed me down like a pile of bricks in a hot air balloon.

I felt as though I were losing my grip on reality. I lost my sense of identity, purpose, and meaning; I was empty. She had ruined me. Drastic measures needed to be taken to find myself again. I began one of the strongest, most backwards journeys to the core of my existence.

I stood in my parents' bathroom staring deeply into my reflection in the mirror. After glowering for a while at the mirror, I began to feel convinced my reflection was another person.

"Who are you?" I asked my reflection, or rather, my reflection asked me. I didn't have an answer. I turned on the clippers in my hand and began to shave the hair from my head. I remember thinking, "This is really strange, Jeremy." It was too late to stop this cathartic experience, though.

The moment became even stranger as I saw my reflection smear toothpaste on his face; he used its adhesiveness to glue clumps of hair to his cheeks.

"Now, who the hell are you?" asked my reflection once more, this time raising his voice. I still had no answer, but I didn't want my reflection to think I was an idiot. I yelled out, "Robert! Robert Frost!"

My reflection shook his head in disapproval. He knew I wasn't Robert, as I would never write about pumpkins.

I left the bathroom and ran into my bedroom. I grabbed a t-shirt, sweatpants, and two thousand dollars in cash. With nothing more on my person, I headed out the door.

Within two hours, I made it to the airport. My bare feet were severely blistered from the walk. I approached the ticket counter and asked the waitress for a ticket to Tibet. I had high hopes of getting advice from the Dalai Lama. Of course, my hopes were shattered when the ticket clerk asked for my passport. I begged and pleaded for her to be merciful to no avail. I would be unable to visit the rare talking Lama.

"I need enlightenment, damn it!" I screamed.

"Security!" yelled the waitress at the counter.

I led a large security guard outside where I instructed him never to let me re-enter the airport; he obeyed me without question. I sat on a bench waiting for lightning to strike me dead, but I quickly deduced it was unlikely, as there was no rain or thunder.

Lana was on my mind, much like in the song about a woman named Georgia. I thought of several times in our relationship where she was troubled by something. I could never recall what upset her, which was not due to any weakness in my memory, but due to the fact that I had often not been listening to her. It begged the question: Why had she been troubled on all those occasions? I had been nothing but happy when I was around her, but could it have been that she had been unhappy with me at times? The thought hit my brain like a horse kicking a child in the face.

A bag boy with a bright yellow and orange vest came out for a smoke break.

"So, you lookin' for some, like, deep spiritual shit?" he asked in his best attempt at the English language.

"I need to figure out who I am," I replied. He puffed his cigarette as he mumbled, "You ever try LSD?" I hadn't, but it was my understanding that it was essentially a stronger version of green tea.

He sold what he called a "tab" of LSD for twenty-five dollars. LSD was a tiny piece of paper the size of a pea. I bought three tabs.

"Do I eat this?" I asked.

He nodded.

"Is it biodegradable?" I asked.

Again, he nodded. I just wanted to be sure it was safe to consume this amount of paper. I placed the three tabs on my tongue. They felt cold and tingly. The bag boy stared at me as though I'd made a huge mistake. He finished his cigarette and left me with the words, "Enjoy, man." I sat on that bench for 20 minutes waiting to be enlightened.

"Pointless," I finally muttered as I stood to begin my walk back to my house. Ten minutes into my walk, I began to feel funny. The wind seemed to be alive, and it was following me home. Mr. Wind, I recall, was a rather unpredictable man. The grass looked and felt like silk. As I walked on the sidewalk, I saw each individual sheath as its own entity. It was as though the sidewalk was a galaxy, and each division was a galaxy within that galaxy. I realize that to a person not influenced by drugs, a sidewalk is not divided up into sheaths, but while under the power of LSD, they were most definitely sheaths.

I observed the vehicles on the road emit beautiful streaks of colored gloss. They welcomed me in as one of their own. I stepped into their world and felt beautiful trumpet music coursing through my body. (It has only recently occurred to me that, at the time, I was walking directly into oncoming traffic.)

A man stopped his car and dragged me into his vehicle. He was an average-looking man except that his eyes glowed with a bright blue light.

"Are you high, man?" he asked. I was fascinated by the resonance of his voice; his adam's apple danced before me like a tribesmen. I remember wanting to take a bite to see if it was as sweet as an apple. I was able to refrain.

I told this gentleman my address, and he flew me home in his rocketship. It took us either three weeks or fourteen minutes to get back to my parents' house. Each attempt I made to reach my parents' doorstep resulted in me teleporting back to the gentleman's car. After what seemed like an hour of this, I opened my eyes to see that I was in my room. This is where things began to get weird.

I lay face up in bed with the sensation that I was floating. I went deaf momentarily, which was quite serene. Suddenly, I sensed the presence of a closeted racist.

"Grandpa?" I called out into the abyss. The presence subsided as soon as my spirit left my body. "Am I dead!?" I shouted in a panic.

"You are everything," replied a deeply ubiquitous being. I had no idea what it meant.

My readers should be aware that this was not an LSD experience I consciously controlled. I genuinely believed I was the savior of the world and that my name was Muhammad Luther King Junior Christ. I sensed my spirit hovering above the universe, judging everyone. I remember having the urge to flood the earth so we could start over; I didn't realize it had been done before.

Suddenly my powers were stripped away. A vacuum in space consumed me at great velocity, breaking the barrier of time. I was taken back through my life. What I saw were distorted versions of reality, but at the time they seemed true. I saw my parents weeping in Dr.Baron's office many years ago after my childhood IQ test, but this time they were not tears of joy. It was as though they wept because I had a mental illness of sorts. I screamed in horror, turning away only to find myself in my school band class. In this version, however, I was unwelcomed as the band teacher. The students were scoffing and mocking me behind my back. Even my close ally, the school principal, was furious with me. I saw myself teaching and referring to the sheet music as shit music.

"What are you doing!? You're insane!" I yelled to my past self in an attempt to get my attention. I ignored me. Everything I knew to be true seemed like a lie. I was convinced I had no traces of mental superiority.

"You're not extraordinary!" declared the ubiquitous voice. I wept loudly as I replied, "I know! I'm delusional!" I felt like I was losing my gifted mind, and finding an ordinary one. My entire life seemed to be a fabrication of my ailing mind.

After hours of arguing and eventually surrendering to the voice, I felt a giant hand made of blazing purple blueberries scoop me up and place me up on the edge of a cliff, where I sobbed uncontrollably for what seemed to be a lifetime. I stripped off my gold-laced garments and tossed them into the horizon. I walked through a maze of crystals and spider webs until standing before a transparent door. A bright light shone through the liquefied crystal barrier. I stood before it in awe. The ubiquitous voice explained that when I made it through this barrier, I would be granted more universal knowledge than ever before. It was an intimidating thought, but I had to know the truth.

I ran at the liquid crystals in a full sprint and leapt like a gazelle jumping over a lion pit. The crystal particles floated like shooting stars around me as I entered the presence of the overpowering light force. This is all I remember.

I awoke to the sound of my screaming mother. When I opened my eyes, I saw an empty carton of blueberries to my right and realized I was lying naked on our back patio. My body was smeared with blueberries and blood. Seeing shattered glass all around me, I deduced that I had run through the glass door in the nude. My mother now stared, frightened and speechless, at me. It was a low point in our relationship.

Sensing she had many awful scenarios running through her mind, I assured her this was just a simple case of her son taking too much LSD. We had a good laugh. More specifically, I had a good laugh, at which point she began weeping.

"I'm a horrible mother!" she said aloud.

"Mom, this was about Lana, I think," I said comfortingly, though it didn't seem to bring her much comfort.

I sat in the kitchen in shorts as my mother stitched my wounds. Her former career as a nurse was finally of use to me.

"What happened with you and Lana?" she asked. I spent a while telling her the complete story.

"Buddy, it sounds like you're in love with her," she said as she poured rubbing alcohol on an open wound.

"I'm not in love, Merilyn. I simply find it difficult to imagine life without her." I told my mom of my failed marriage proposal to Lana. Her reply was, "You were sixteen years old." I have no idea why she made such an obvious statement.

My mother encouraged me to speak to Lana. What she didn't understand was that I was feeling desperate, and I had promised myself long ago to never do anything out of desperation. Furthermore, a genius never begs. After all, why should they? They have everything they could want in their brain cavity. Thus, since Lana wanted to move on, I did, too.

"I'm taking a long trip," I said.

"Why?"

"Boredom." In reality, I was anything but bored.

"Darling, what about Lana?" she asked.

I placed my finger over her lips and softly whispered, "Shhhh... we're moving on from this." My mom simply accepted this.

"Okay, where are you going?" she asked.

"Bangladesh," I replied. She asked me why I was going to Asia. My mother was clearly not a geographist.

I vowed never to take LSD again; I vowed it again the next time I accidentally took it. That time I awoke on the stage of a Nickelback concert; their music sounds horrific while on LSD. LSD is supposed to reveal more of ourselves to us, yet every time I took it I was absolutely convinced I was mentally ill and exceptionally unintelligent.

After my first LSD experience, I was relieved to regain consciousness as the savant that I am. The person I believed I was while on acid was a sad version of myself. He was a creature so out of touch with reality that his daily existence was an attempt to fool himself into feeling special. I never wanted to see that distorted version of myself again. Fortunately, the whole experience ultimately led me to realize what I really wanted out of life: seclusion.

CHAPTER 12: INCOMMUNICADO

"Loneliness is loyal; it's always there when you need a friend."

—Jeremy Jude

Many humans despise the idea of being alone, but I have always been fascinated by the hermits of the world; they purposely remove themselves from society as a religious discipline. With Lana out of my foreseeable future, I decided to hermitize myself as a way to adjust to the idea that I'd likely die alone in a nursing home.

I decided against Bangladesh as my destination, as I was in search of alone time; the worst place to go for alone time is one of the most densely populated countries in the world. Instead, after some profound self-reflection, I decided to take up hiking around the United States.

Hiking became a new obsession of mine. At first, hitch-hiking was my favorite form, but it lacked the privacy I was desiring; when one hitch-hikes, they are basically forced to talk to the driver. Anyone who plans to hitch-hike should know there are a lot of strange people out there. (Also, do not attempt to hitch-hike in Detroit.) I spent weeks hitch-hiking before someone told me about nature hiking. It sounded closer to my vision.

A truck driver dropped me off at a sporting goods store in Colorado, where I used my lawyer dad's borrowed credit card to buy the best hiking supplies I could find.

I was forcibly asked to leave the first trail I hiked on, as it was considered private property.

"Sir, this is a golf course," said a gentleman in a cart. I was furious since I had just erected my tent near the eighteenth hole. Within a few days, I found the appropriate trails. A man I hitched a hike with dropped me off near the start of a known trail. I gave him a power bar as a tip and began my journey into the unknown, man-made trails.

The first hour of hiking was disenchanting. As it turns out, hiking is just walking long distances with a heavy backpack strapped to you. While the scenery was beautiful, it quickly became repetitive. After a while, my legs began to itch; I deduced its source was the patch of poison ivy I had walked through while taking a shortcut. I wondered who had discovered that poison ivy isn't edible. There must have been a caveman who served a poison ivy salad to his group; of course, he probably introduced it as an ivy salad at the time.

Three hours into the mind-numbing hike, my cell phone rang. It was my mother calling for the tenth time that month. I answered due to boredom.

"Talk to me," I said.

"Oh, thank goodness!" She sounded overly eager to hear my voice. "Buddy, are you alright? Where are you?"

"Hiking in Colorado."

"You're in Colorado?"

"Hiking..."

"Well, we haven't heard from you in over a month." I was starting to regret answering the phone. My mother was impeding my solitude.

"I sent an email," I said.

"That was over a month ago, sweetheart."

"Touché, I suppose."

"Okay...well, just be safe, alright, buddy? Keep in touch with us."

"No, that defeats the purpose of all this," I explained.

"What purpose, bud?"

My cell phone beeped in my ear. I looked at it and saw the words "4% battery remaining." I hung up the phone.

I continued down the path for hours, until the monotony of my footsteps lulled me deep into my thoughts. For five hours and twenty-two minutes, I lost all track of time. My mind played out a fun daydream in which I was an Egyptian servant called into the throneroom of Queen Nefertiti due to her sexual attraction to me. Nefertiti met me in her time period, but when I traveled back to the present, she summoned her god Aten to send her to the future to be with me. We fell in love, but all the while, her jealous husband, Pharaoh Akhenaten, chased us through time in attempts to destroy our love. Had I known at the time that this sort of subject would have become so popular, I would have written a novel about my adventure-filled daydream. It would have been a time travel novel titled *Nefertiti's Kiss*. Perhaps I'll write it once I'm done writing my memoirs.

The sun began to set, and I was nowhere near a rest stop. I had passed one hours ago, but it was full of snobby hikers warning me that there wasn't another rest stop for hours. They strongly advised me to spend the night with them, which I found odd. I was already suspicious of their motives, and I didn't like being told what to do, especially by hikers.

Soon the birds gave their chirping duties to the crickets, the moon traded places with the sun, and I took off in a jog hoping to find any traces of civilization before evil spirits caught me. While I don't believe evil spirits are that interested in haunting humans, or that they even exist, the eerie darkness had me convinced something was after me. This was undoubtedly the result the horror film marathon I partook in once for nineteen straight hours.

Fifteen minutes into my jog, I saw a shadowy figure on the trail several yards in front of me. It had the shape of a large, demonic creature. Imagine a gorilla standing upright, but having longer legs, a smaller upper body, and a walk like a human; that is the figure I saw. My survival training took over, and I darted off the trail, into the woods. I sprinted as fast as I could, for as long as I could, until I stepped into a muddy creek. My socks and shoes were instantly soaked by the twelve-inch-deep sludge. At the second splash, I abruptly halted and stood panting in the middle of the creek, eyeing my surroundings. It was dark, but there was just enough moonlight for me to see I was fucked.

The way back to the trail was unclear, and I had been running for quite some time. I pulled out my cell phone and turned it on, hoping to make use of the last remaining drop of energy from it. The battery blinked as I sent a text to my mom: *SOS Lana*. As soon as it sent, my phone shut off. The chances of my mom knowing what SOS meant were slim, but I knew Lana would interpret my message; she was the one who had taught me its meaning years ago.

It takes a true man to be courageous in these situations, but an even truer man to be vulnerable enough to cry. I sat on a log by the creek, removing my muddy socks as I wept uncontrollably; this time, I'm afraid, it wasn't a stoic man cry.

There were rumors of bear attacks near the trails, but I knew the bears would be warded off by my bitter tears. My howls competed with those of a distant coyote until it stopped; even the coyote recognized that I was the one with real problems. That night, I cried myself to sleep. Early in the morning, I laughed myself to wake; it seemed appropriate, though exceedingly forced.

When I awoke, all I saw were trees hovering above me in the morning mist. The sky was barely visible, as the trees had created a shadowy environment beneath them. I walked steadily through the shadow of death, hoping to find the trail I had veered off of the night before. I had learned a tracking technique from the children's story "Hansel and Gretel," in which Hansel leaves a trail of breadcrumbs on the path. Alas, the technique only works if someone has already left a trail of crumbs. I wandered through the forest until the sun began to set again.

"This isn't right," I said.

"What's not right, Jeremy?" I asked. I suppose I'd become my own Wilson volleyball, as seen in the indie film *Cast Away*; It's a movie about the quirky relationship between a man and a volleyball on a deserted island. Wilson's character is the strong, silent type, brilliantly contrasted by the Tom Cruisesque energy of actor Tom Hanks.

"Why haven't we found the trail yet?" I asked in an animated, slightly irritated voice. My cold reply was simply, "We should erect the tent for the night." I knew I was right, but spending another night in those forests was a hard pill to swallow, and I always gagged when I tried to swallow pills. I sat on a rock and stared blankly at another rock. I looked down at my grimy hands. Something about the dirt covering my usually clean hands triggered something inside me. I wept for thirty minutes, hydrated for two, ate a powerbar for five, and got up to assemble the tent.

The orange hue of the setting sun was timing me, like my despondent coach in gym class. I wanted to be inside the tent before dark. It's illogical, but the inside of a tent gives me the illusion of safety. In reality, the walls of a tent can be easily penetrated by a bear claw, a falling tree, or the machete of a killer.

I made it into the tent just before a heavy rain began to pour. I had a flashlight with no batteries. My only source of light was the frequent flashes of lighting diffused by the tent's material. My mother once told me a flash of lightning was just God taking a picture of the earth. If this was true, it would have been nice for God to send the pictures to a rescue team to show them my location. I closed my eyes as I listened to the sounds of the thunder and rain. I imagined myself as a pirate below the deck of a ship.

Before I knew it, morning had come. In nature, birds are the parents that wake their children early on Saturdays. My back ached from having fallen asleep on the flashlight. I sat up groggily and searched through my backpack for coffee. It had been a fantasy of mine to drink coffee in a tent alone ever since I'd read a short story by Hemingway about a man drinking coffee in a tent near a river.

I pulled out the tin of ground coffee and scooped a spoonful directly into a tin cup. I recalled an argument I'd had with Lana regarding the use of coffee filters; I could not remember which side of the argument I had been on. With the spoon, I stirred as I poured fresh water from my canteen. From my bag, I grabbed six sugar packets and tore them open into the coffee. The sugar always made the bitter taste of coffee tolerable. I held a cigar lighter under the cup until it heated the drink. After a sip of the lukewarm coffee, I stepped out of my tent and dumped the rest of the coffee on the ground; it was atrocious. For the first time, I understood why they referred to it as ground coffee.

I packed my meager belongings and began my daily trek. Morale was low, so I decided to give myself a motivational speech: "If you don't find civilization by tonight, you're probably going to die out here."

On that particular day, I walked at a faster pace to cover more ground, optimistic that I would find a way out. That night, I cried myself to sleep again. I cried again the next night, and the one after that, and the next. Five more horrendous nights passed without hope. My food supply was nearly halfway gone, but my water supply was endless, as the man at the supermarket convinced me to buy several bottles of germicidal tablets that made river water safe to drink. I thought he was an idiot for making me buy so many bottles, but I was beginning to see his side of things.

Regardless of external amenities, things were bleak. As I walked, I grew weaker and weaker. The bones in my face ached from exhaustion. After miles of hiking, I unfastened my backpack, stood on a log, and shouted, "HEEEELP!!!" It echoed across the wilderness. This was the first time in my life I had ever asked for help.

"HEEELP!!!" I shouted again. The word faded into the wind. I stepped off the log, uncertain of what to do next; Nature has a way of crushing even the most brilliant men. I vividly remember sitting on the ground and embracing my large backpack. Tears began streaming down my cheeks as I rocked the backpack back and forth.

"It's okay, sweetie. Everything's okay," I told the backpack, though I doubt he believed me. I fell asleep in his arms (or straps, if you prefer).

I was jolted out of my sleep by a tickling sensation crawling up my forearm. I didn't want to open my eyes, but I knew I had to. There was a hairy, one-inch spider crawling up my arm. I cupped my hand over it, failing to realize I'd trapped it between my hand and my forearm. I felt its fangs pierce deep into my flesh. Frantically, I waved my arm around until it loosened its grip. It tumbled to the ground, then crawled away as though it had done this a thousand times. I was disgusted to think that it probably had.

My ears were ringing, my heart beating fast. I watched as the skin around the bite mark began to swell. I began to hyperventilate as the harsh reality sunk in. I sat on the dirt floor in a nervous sweat, knowing it was time to write down my final words. I scrambled through my backpack until finding paper and a pencil. As sweat dripped down my forehead, this is what I wrote:

I've had a good life. I've been a psychiatrist, musician, restaurant owner, college professor, father, chief of police, model, friend, adviser, professional gambler, drug user, and lover. I never predicted I'd die at twenty-two, but I can say I've already had a full life. Mom, Dad, Candice, and Leo, I love you with all my brain. (I can't use my heart right now, as my bloodstream is full of poison.)

I have but two regrets: The first is allowing myself to be bitten by a deadly spider, and the second is Lana. I regret not pursuing her. I regret moving on without trying to win her back. I should have gone to Italy. Please tell her I have always loved her. No, wait, don't tell her. It would only cause her more anguish surrounding my death. Tell her I died in the arms of another lover. No, don't tell her that. It could also cause her pain. Just invite her to my funeral party, but tell her not to bring her new boyfriend, if she has one. Change that, he can come, too, I suppose. I don't want her to think I was the jealous type. No, actually...

The tip of my pencil broke. I desperately dumped the contents of my backpack onto the ground in search of another pencil. Never have I been more desperate for a pencil, or any other item for that matter. Upon realizing there was not another pencil, I threw myself on the ground and screamed louder than I ever had before or ever have since.

With nothing left to do, I lay face up on the ground, waiting for the poison to reach the chambers of my heart. It's strange, the things one thinks about before death. I remembered a diner I'd been to once as a child. I remembered watching a cook toss eight raw patties on the grill and press on each one with his spatula. As a child, I had no opinions about the way he cooked those patties. I found great delight in the simplicity of that moment. With a smile on my face, I closed my eyes and began to release my spirit from my body, gently fading into the darkness of the abyss.

"Hey, I found him!" shouted who I thought was an angel at the time. I sat up and opened my eyes to see that I was face to face with a sloppy hound dog. Its leash was attached to a sloppy man in an orange vest. I realized I'd only fallen asleep.

"Hey, are you okay?" asked the man. I held up my forearm to my eyeline, wondering why the bite hadn't killed me yet. I was reminded of a news story I'd read as a child wherein a youth was bitten by a spider during a school field trip. He fell asleep, just as I had; upon waking, he discovered that he no longer needed glasses and that he had taken on the characteristics of the very spider who bit him.

The man in the orange vest led me to the search party, where dozens of men and women in orange vests were gathered. As we walked towards them, they began applauding me for my heroics. I was led to a woman wearing an orange vest and latex gloves. She introduced herself to me as a medic, but upon examining my bite, she claimed it wasn't a deadly spider that bit me.

"Just because one person is immune, does not mean the spider is not deadly," I said. My explanation fell on deaf ears, mainly because she was deaf.

That night, I spoke on the phone with my parents from a hotel room.

"I need to stay here for a week," I explained. My mother wept as she begged me to come home. My father told me he knew I stole his credit card. They had gotten more concerned when charges had stopped showing up on it. Under the circumstances, he told me I could use it to buy a plane ticket.

"Is Lana still in Italy?" I asked.

"Yes," replied my mother. "She's been calling every day asking about you."

"Why was she asking about me?"

"Well, to see if they'd found you."

"Okay, good. Well, have a good night! I have things to do," I said, then hung up the phone. I had managed to survive the deadly spider bite; now I needed to do something to resolve my only other regret.

CHAPTER 13: BONJOURNO PRINCIPESSA!

"When in Rome, never do as the Romans do. In case you haven't noticed, their empire eventually collapsed."

—Jeremy Jude

A week later, I took a flight from Colorado to Florence, Italy. My intentions were to propose to my soul mate Lana for the second time. Before leaving Colorado, I bought a loose diamond with my lawyer dad's credit card. It wasn't the diamond I'd hoped to give Lana, but it was all I could afford at the time.

When I landed in Italy, the first thing I did was go to a florist where I bought flowers for Lana. After that, I had a jeweler embed the diamond into a gold ring. I drove my rental moped to Lana's university. It was complete with cobblestone grounds, stone buildings, a bell tower, and a misplaced fountain I nearly crashed into whilst admiring the aforementioned bell tower. The windy ride had disintegrated my bouquet of flowers, leaving a trail of petals like in the children's story of "Hansel and Gretel." Ironic, since I had needed a trail like that back when I had been lost in the forest.

I parked my moped on the hip of a statue of a naked fellow with strong muscles; I knew he could handle it. When I turned around, there walked a tan, more matured Lana heading to class.

"Lana!" I shouted. She gawked at me with an open mouth and, I hoped, an open heart. She looked confused, but also more beautiful than ever. "Bonjourno, principessa!" I shouted, extending the disfigured bouquet for her to see. The greeting was a romantic reference from the Italian movie *Life Is Beautiful*. While that movie was terribly tragic and mainly took place in a concentration camp, the first portion was very charming.

She marched towards me looking a little more fiery than I had expected, and I worried that quoting a tragic movie had offended her.

"What are you doing here?" she said. "Your parents called me worried sick about you! They said you never arrived home!"

"Hmmm...I suppose I should have told them I rerouted to Florence."

I deduced that proposing to Lana in her current state would not go well. My new objective was to get Lana to stop being angry with me.

"I'm sorry. I was being selfish," I said, knowing this was likely what she needed to hear; I admit I had no feelings of remorse. Empathy has always been a struggle for me; one basic requirement for empathy is relating to others. Having a brain that is the equivalent of five normal brains, though, would make empathy difficult for anyone.

"Is there a mall we can go to? I need to buy some flip flops," I said.

"I think I need some time to process, Jeremy."

"How long? Ten, fifteen minutes?" I asked. She thought about it long and hard, until finally saying,

"Some of my friends are watching a soccer match at my apartment at two o'clock. I live in Apartment 14 across the street. You can meet us then." I told her I'd be there as I struggled to get my helmet over my beard. Since I had started hiking, I'd let it grow long and unmanageable to embrace the fashion of a man belonging to wilderness and seclusion. Lana walked to her next class without saying goodbye as the bell from a nearby tower bellowed solemnly.

Creating a romantic situation was going to be difficult with all her friends around. The best solution would be to seduce the entire group so as to create a collective romantic environment, at which point biological forces would take over and we would pair off with our corresponding mates.

I drove to a tiny market where I bought six bottles of wine, a bouquet of bread, salami, bruschetta, olive oil, and a bottle of chocolate liquor. The middle-aged woman at the checkout counter talked a lot as she put my groceries in paper bags. Her excessive smiles, hand gestures, and laughter were signs that she was romantically interested in me.

"So sorry, I'm getting married soon," I told her before heading out the door.

Holding this quantity of groceries whilst driving a moped proved to be a difficult task. I arrived at my destination with only five bottles of wine, salami, and a bottle of chocolate liquor.

I knocked on the door, and Lana let me into her apartment. The walls were pure concrete, and the windows extended to the floor. She introduced me to her friends one by one. First, I met Freddie, a blonde-haired, blue-eyed Italian gentleman. His real name was Facundo, but I didn't care to learn how to pronounce that. Then I met Lana's roommate, Sandra, a "hottie with a body," as the term goes, that I didn't notice because I was there for Lana. I knew Sandra would be attractive enough to keep Freddie's attention away from Lana for the evening. My only other threat was named Pablo; he wasn't much of a threat, though. He seemed more interested in the soccer match on TV than in any girl in the room. Lastly, and perhaps leastly, I was introduced to Sofia, the all-too-hyper friend every female seems to have. She was clearly interested in Pablo, as she spent most of her time watching him watch the soccer match. I began to refer to Pablo as Van Gogh because she talked his ear off, and, I assumed, he possessed some kind of mental oddity that allowed him to tolerate the talking.

Freddie, hot Sandra, Lana, and I sat at the kitchen table drinking wine and eating. I managed to discreetly incorporate my many rehearsed jokes into the conversation. Lana laughed mildly at three of my eight jokes. Freddie laughed at five of my eight jokes. Hot Sandra laughed loudly at all eight jokes. At one point, Sandra got up to use the restroom. Lana leaned over to me and said, "She really likes you; you should ask her on a date." It's amazing how a compliment, in the right context, can be the most devastating thing a person could ever say. When Sandra returned to the table, I promptly excused myself and locked myself in the restroom.

I looked at myself in the mirror. "Think!" I commanded. I needed a brilliant, non-self-sabotaging idea to attract Lana. It was around this time I first began to realize that there was a very destructive part of myself that reared its head in times of disillusionment. I needed the genius self to take control. The conversation between these two parts of myself went as follows:

DESTRUCTIVE SELF

Clearly 'tis over. I say you grab hot Sandra and kiss her wildly so as to utterly, irreparably destroy all rapport you had with Lana.

GENIUS SELF

I object. There are three bottles of wine left. Drink them in under five minutes to impress Lana. If you fail, you will at least be incapable of remembering your heartache.

DESTRUCTIVE SELF

No, that won't work. You must become the alpha and omega male. Walk up to Freddie and say, "Did you just call my future wife a bitch!?" Then punch him unapologetically in the left nostril. He's a very nice guy. He'll forgive you, and Lana will think of you as her knight in shining armor.

GENIUS SELF

Violence isn't the answer! Unless, of course, you're capable of fighting both Freddie and Van Gogh. This would make an unforgettable impression in Lana's brain. Perhaps Destructive Self was onto something.

DESTRUCTIVE SELF

Why, thank you, darling. Might I take it a step further?

GENIUS SELF

By all means!

DESTRUCTIVE SELF

I don't want to step on your toes here...

GENIUS SELF

No, no, no! I insist.

DESTRUCTIVE SELF

What if we combine all the aforementioned ideas into a single sequence of events?

GENIUS SELF

My god, you are the real genius!

DESTRUCTIVE SELF

Oh, please. You contributed a great amount. If anything, this idea was the result of our chemistry and collaborative efforts!

In reality, it had been my destructive self talking to my destructive self; my genius self sometimes malfunctions when emotionally overburdened. I opened the door and marched towards the kitchen to execute my destructive sequence of events. But I was maturing; My true genius self whispered faintly, "You've already hurt her." In an instant, I realized I just wanted that adorable female to live a happy life, with or without me. I never wanted to cause her pain again. Was it empathy I was experiencing? Unlikely.

I entered the kitchen like Charlie Brown, who clearly suffered from chronic depression. There stood the group holding up a cake with lit candles for me.

"What's this for?" I asked. As it turned out, it was my twenty-third birthday; this explained my sudden increase in maturity. I was impressed that Lana remembered what I had completely forgotten. I was still feeling twenty-two.

"Make a wish!" exclaimed Freddie. I know they say a wish is

nullified if you vocalize it, but I've found no scientific evidence to back up this claim. I blew out the flames upon the candles and opened my mouth to wish. Out of the corner of my eye, I noticed a nervous expression on Lana's face. Perhaps she thought I was going to wish for us to get back together again; I wished this aloud at my birthday party several years earlier, and she didn't seem to like it then, either.

"I wish to eat cake with friends," I said.

In less than a minute, my wish came true. I never make a wish that might not come true; as a genius, I cannot deal with uncertainties. Consequently, all my birthday wishes have come true, except the year I foolishly wished for a go-kart. I'd had a dream about getting a go-kart the night before that birthday and had been certain it was a sign. I did not get a go-kart for my birthday, and it was the worst birthday I've ever had.

Lana's whole demeanor seemed to change after my wish. We spent the rest of the afternoon talking and laughing as a group. We ate tiramisu cake. We watched a boring game of soccer. We drank alcoholic wine. It got late.

"So, where are you staying?" asked Lana.

"A hotel," I replied.

"What hotel?" asked Freddie.

"Any," I replied.

"You haven't booked a hotel?" asked hot Sandra.

"No," I replied. I marveled at how the topic of my lodging had become a group debate.

"Hotels will be full. Art convention in town," muttered Van Gogh.

"I'll find a hostel," I said.

"No! Sei Americano!" screeched Sofia.

"That's true, hostels aren't the safest," said Lana.

"But I'm a full grown adult," I explained.

"He can stay with me," said Freddie.

"Are you sure?" asked Lana.

"Of course!" exclaimed Freddie.

It was settled.

On our way out, Lana invited me to go swimming with the group at Van Gogh's grandparents' vineyard on the countryside the next morning. I promptly accepted. Freddie and I walked to my rental moped; Sofia and Van Gogh were supposed to be his ride home, but they drove off without telling us.

"Oh, I forget something inside," said Freddie as he turned to go back to the apartment. As I waited, I realized I had forgotten my socks and shoes inside. When I opened the door to the apartment, I was shocked to see the beast with two lips; Freddie and Lana were kissing each other goodbye with their mouths. Italy had turned Lana into a floozy.

As they kissed, Lana had her eyes wide open, staring into Freddie's eyelids. It was at this point that I knew Lana was deeply in love with Freddie; she was so in love with him she couldn't take her gaze off him for even a moment. I was sure now that Lana had moved on, and since my new objective was to never hurt her again, I decided to do my best to move on as well.

I sat on the moped pretending I saw nothing. Freddie walked out with an air of secret satisfaction. And I do redact the part where I called Lana a floozy; She's a saint.

"You want I drive?" Freddie asked me upon noticing the multiple bags of groceries resting on my lap.

"Knock yourself out," I said, secretly meaning it literally.

The frustrating part was that Freddie was not only as handsome as a Vogue model; he was also an extremely magnanimous guy. He was the kind of man that girls asked out on a date. When girls dreamt of prince charming, he was the default template in their imaginations. The expression "he could get away with murder" would likely hold true for him; I'm sure police would let him go and apologize for the inconvenience. His mere presence made girls swoon; I even felt a bit faint the first time I stared into those beautiful blue eyes. I hate to admit, he was so breathtaking that even Nefertiti would have dated him. I thought he could be the protagonist in my next novel, *Nefertiti's Kiss*.

As Freddie steered the moped down the cobblestone roads I barely hung on to his waist. Frankly, I didn't want to touch my ex-girlfriend's new boyfriend. Ergo, my helmet saved my skull three times on the way to Freddie's apartment.

The next morning, Freddie and I rode in his car to pick up Lana and Sandra. I sat in the back seat to avoid sitting next to Freddie. The girls were waiting outside Lana's apartment when we drove up. It was peculiar that Lana sat in the backseat with me; Sandra sat in the front with Freddie. I deduced it was all for appearances; it was evident to me that Freddie and Lana wanted to sit together. My ashy heart didn't particularly want to be near either of them.

"Lana, trade seats with Sandra, please. I'm allergic to your deoderant." She shot me a curious look.

"It's the same deodorant I've always worn around you," she said, and she was right.

"I'm allergic to your perfume, then," I rebutted. We both knew she wasn't wearing perfume, but she traded places with Sandra anyway; Sandra was thrilled. I decided then to make my new objective to seduce Sandra to distract me from my covetous feelings towards

Freddie. Not only was it a mature decision, but Sandra was also beautiful and charming, so I stood to benefit, should I meet the objective. Her savory brown eyes, her olive oil complexion, and her silky brown hair were further complemented by her strong Italian accent and raspy voice.

We arrived at Van Gogh's grandparents' farmhouse next to the vineyard. Van Gogh and Sofia met us on the dirt road then led us to a parking place in front of the house. Freddie removed his key from the ignition, and the resulting silence felt like a gun marking the beginning of a grueling race. I deduced the next few hours would, indeed, be grueling and would consist of Lana and Freddie attempting to spare my already hurt feelings by denying their urges to touch and/or be near one another while Sofia and I played an endless game filled with stressful amounts of sexual tension. I didn't want this.

"Kiss each other if you'd like," I said to Lana and Freddie. They looked at each other, almost in shock. I turned my attention to Sandra, who was already staring at me.

"Let's take a tour of the pool, yes?" I said. She followed me out of the car like a heat-seeking missile following the Human Torch. We greeted Van Gogh and Sofia. A cool breeze traveled across the quiet orchard just to make my acquaintance; at that point, I knew the day would be better.

After swimming, we sat next to the pool sipping coffee and enjoying the pastries Van Gogh's grandmother had baked for us. Sandra and I sat close together. Next to us sat Lana and Freddie, and beside them sat Sofia and Van Gogh.

"What happened to your arm?" Lana asked me. The spider bite hadn't completely healed yet. As I told them the story of my near-death experience in Colorado, Sandra slowly began leaning her entire body against mine; I rather enjoyed hot Sandra's physical way of listening to stories. Lana didn't seem to care for it; she had that hilarious furrowed brow she subconsciously expresses when hiding the fact that she's upset.

A wrinkly, old man whom I presumed to be Van Gogh's grandfather emerged from the house in a Speedo suit and sandals to tell Freddie he had a phone call. Freddie took the call inside. Sandra leaned in close to me and whispered into my ear, "Jeremy, we go walk the orchards?" She playfully grabbed hold of my waist, which, I must admit, was arousing.

"Lana, would you mind tossing me my jeans?" I asked. As she picked them up I heard a clinking noise. No one else seemed to notice.

Lana picked the diamond ring up off the floor. We locked eyes, neither of us saying a word. Just then, Freddie emerged from the house gleefully. Lana reflexively hid the ring behind her back as though she'd done something wrong.

"Lana, the museum called! They has an opening today!" exclaimed Freddie, clasping his hands together with delight. I was fascinated by his mannerisms; I clasped my hands together and imitated his thick Italian accent. Hot Sandra threw her head back as she burst into laughter. She put her hand on my thigh as she struggled to catch her breath. It really wasn't that funny.

"But not everyone will be able to go," said Lana to Freddie.

"No, we all go! I got six tickets for us!" he exclaimed. Everyone minus me seemed thrilled by the news. What was so exciting about visiting an art museum in Italy? I could have seen all the paintings for free on Google Images.

Sandra and I carpooled with Van Gogh and Sofia, which was unpleasant. Sofia had her hand over Van Gogh's stick-shifting hand the entire way to the museum. There was a brief moment when I thought she was operating the gears, but it was an optical illusion. Ahead of our car were Freddie and Lana; Lana still had my diamond ring, but I trusted her not to steal it. After all, it was meant for her anyway.

It was a hot day in Florence; it was the kind of day to be near a pool, yet there we stood in a long line outside the art museum.

"Damn it, Freddie, I thought you had tickets," I said sternly; Sandra laughed.

"They takes only one group at a time," explained Freddie.

"Banksy would never make anyone stand in line for his street art," I muttered; Sandra again laughed. Meanwhile, Van Gogh and Sofia were passionately kissing against the guardrail. There's something about passionate couples that makes them think they're invisible in hot tubs, pools, fairgrounds, movie theatres, public restrooms, parks, beaches, and long lines. At least it was something to watch as we waited.

Our tour guide was a fifty-something, skinny gentleman with a thin mustache and messy, gray hair; I liked him at first. He led us into the museum to the first painting and boastfully imparted his vast knowledge of the painting into my uninterested ears. The painting was of two naked angels and a naked, bearded gentleman. It was not the work of a genius, as geniuses often choose more original concepts than this. I'd seen similar paintings in the cathedral in Argentina.

"Pretentious," I muttered.

"Scusi?" asked our tour guide, to which I cleverly replied, "You're escusied."

He didn't get it. We moved on to the next painting three steps away, and the tour guide began another divulgence about the history of this boring painting. It was very similar to the previous painting both in style and idiocy. Sofia listened with her hand in Van Gogh's back pocket; it's an irrelevant detail but one I regrettably remember.

I glanced down the hall at all the other pretentious paintings. There were thirty-two total, none better than the first two. I leaned over to Freddie and asked, "Will this tour guide be giving us a history of all the paintings?"

"Of course!" he replied.

I began walking to the end of the hall.

"Scusi, signore!" exclaimed the nervous tour guide, whom I ignored. Lana asked me where I was going.

"I don't know. Where's the exit?" I asked. The tour guide pointed me to a door nearby.

"I go with him!" stated Sandra to the group. Her excuse was that I "didn't know the Florence area." Before leaving, we made arrangements to meet up with the group at a gelato shop after they finished their tour of purgatory.

Sandra and I sauntered to a public park where we spent the entire time making out ferociously on a bench; I don't think anyone saw us since the children were busy playing, and the parents were busy removing their children from the playground area. By the end of our hour-long session, the park was almost empty.

After that session, we had both worked up an appetite for gelato. We walked to the shop and sat at a small table outside as we waited for the group. I took this opportunity to ask hot Sandra out on a date; she was ecstatic.

"Let's celebrate with gelato, shall we?" I said. She suggested we wait for the others to arrive. This is when I laughed in her face; I thought she was kidding. Who established the rules of etiquette, anyway? Who is so important that all must cease their eating habits for them? I subscribe to the idea that it's far ruder to make others wait on you to be nourished. Making others wait on you is acceptable only if you're the one bringing the food.

I kissed Sandra on her Italian lips and stepped into the gelato shop without her. A friendly old lady behind the counter greeted me with a smile. Once I established that she spoke English, I placed my order. "I'll have a cookie dough gelato," I said.

"No cookie dough gelato," She replied.

"Then I'll have peanut butter cup."

"No peanut cup."

"Cookies n' cream?"

"No cookie creams."

"Rocky road."

"No rocky."

"Then just give me whatever the hell you do have."

"Twenty flavors," she said, pointing at all the flavors.

"I'll have the green one!"

"Pistachio or mint?"

"Surprise me."

"Pistachio!" she said with a grin.

"I hate pistachios!"

The tender lady handed me a gelato cone with the mint flavor. I turned to see that Lana and Freddie were outside already chatting with Sandra, who was smiling about something. She pointed at me as she spoke with Lana; Lana faked a smile. I stepped outside to greet them.

Sandra signaled for me to sit next to her as though I were a lost child at an amusement park; she was not yet aware that I hated being treated like a little boy. She wrapped her arm around mine as she kissed me on the cheek. My main concern at this point was the gelato tilting in my hand. Lana forced a smile as she asked me, "Aren't you leaving in a few days, Jeremy?"

"Yeah, why?"

"Oh...is Sandra aware of this?"

"It is just casual," added Sandra, which was news to me. I realize long distance relationships are often fruitless, and though I would have never moved to Italy for her, I wanted Sandra and me to fool ourselves into believing it could work out; eventually, we would grow deeply attached to one another until finally reaching a devastating breakup. By the end of this grueling process, I would have at least known I was capable of loving a non-Lana girl, meaning I would have matured to the point of moving on with my life.

Lana had the idea to go to a coffee shop; I love coffee shops. She leaned over to Sandra and said sweetly, "You don't have to go if you don't want to, Sandra. I know you're not a big fan of those type of places,"

"No. Is okay. I go," replied Sandra with a huge smile. These girls were suddenly in a great mood as their conversation about coffee continued.

"Are you sure? You won't offend us," said Lana.

"I'm sure," replied Sandra, "I want to go."

Lana chuckled playfully, Sandra chuckled playfully, and, inevitably, I chuckled playfully. Although I love coffee shops, I hadn't initially been in the mood to drink coffee, but after seeing Lana and Sandra's enthusiasm, I was all in.

"I'm all in! let's get coffee!" I exclaimed.

Out of nowhere, Sandra playfully leaned in and whispered something rather sensual to me; I giggled, which Lana instantly took note of.

"We're not gossiping about you," I assured Lana, to which she replied, "I didn't think you were." Sandra whispered something else – this time it was something unsuitable for books, television, movies, or the general public. I was aware Sandra was not the most sexually reserved girl, but I had no idea how far her lack of reservation actually extended. Even E.L. James would have been shocked by Sandra's suggestion.

"Are you okay?" asked Freddie upon noticing my pale expression; I was not. What Sandra whispered left me feeling squeamish. I'd rather not disclose even the slightest hint of what Sandra said, mostly because it still grosses me out, and even mentioning blood causes me to lose consciousness.

"Who...let's...are we going to get coffee?" I asked, still feeling a bit wobbly.

"You all go," said Sandra, now avoiding eye contact with me.

"You sure?" asked Lana. Sandra feigned a smile as she nodded. As we stood, Lana turned to Freddie.

"Are you coming, Facu?" she asked him.

"Eh...you both go catch up," he said with a gentle smile. She smiled back, but not as sincerely. I could always tell when Lana faked a smile, a laugh, or a good mood. I never did figure out when she was faking being upset with me, as she always seemed pretty convincing.

Lana and I walked several blocks to a coffee shop, neither of us talking along the way. I had missed that comfortable silence we used to share. In the coffee shop, Lana ordered her usual cappuccino. I ordered tonic water. I followed her up the stairs out to a patio overlooking the city. She looked stunning in her sundress. We sat at a table and smiled a friendly smile at each other.

"You have to try a sip of this," she said as she handed me her cup. I took a sip and was unimpressed.

"Too strong," I said.

"Oh, I forgot, I still have your ring in my purse," she added as she reached for the ring.

"Could you hold on to it for now? I'm afraid of it falling from my pocket again."

She placed it back in her purse.

"I think it's great you're with Freddy," I said.

"You do?" she asked. I actually hated that she was with Freddy, but I realized I could do nothing to change that, unless I resorted to darker schemes.

"He's very handsome," I told her. She stared at her coffee momentarily.

"Your mom read me your text. Did she tell you?" she asked, rather reservedly.

"What text?"

"SOS Lana."

"Ah, yes!"

"I was the one that told her you were in serious trouble."

"Thank you."

She looked at me in a way that reminded me of how she looked at me years ago, standing in her parents' driveway, right before we kissed for the first time. I was remaining as stoic as I could, so as to avoid professing my love for her right then and there. It seemed as though she were about to say something remarkable to me.

"Where are you going after Italy?" she asked. I told her I was going home. "Will you be there in six months?" she asked.

"Yes, I will," I said with certainty. Judging by her reaction, it seemed an unbelievable concept to her.

"You mean you *think* you will be there, or will you actually be there?" she asked again.

"I will be there," I replied. The rest of the conversation was laced with avoidance of larger topics and hidden feelings, but it was still pleasant.

I decided to leave Italy that night. My relationship with Sandra was now questionable at best, and Lana was unavailable. That evening, I wrote Freddie a thank you note, which I left in his bed, specifically in his mouth. It wasn't my original plan, but when I knocked over his vase upon entering his room, I realized how deep of a sleeper he was. It was only natural at that point to further investigate how deep his sleep extended. I slapped him for good measure but found his sleep threshold and thought it best to exit the premises quickly.

I sped off on my rental moped, driving past the university, then to Lana's apartment building, where I stopped my moped in the quiet street and gazed up toward her apartment. Rain started to drip on my helmet. I saw a light on in her room, and for an instant considered going to her doorstep in the pouring rain as a final strategy to win her back. Rain leads to increased romantic feelings in women, but I'm unsure why. I've heard there's a strong correlation between wetness and a girl's libidinal urges. But it was futile, at that moment, for me to even try; Lana was not in love with me. I decided to temporarily shut down my emotions and speed off on my moped. I knew neither of us could be negatively affected by my maneuver.

I headed back to the United States empty-handed in multiple ways: Hot Sandra and I were done, I never proposed to Lana, and I had left my engagement ring in Lana's purse. She would be returning to the United States in six months, so I would get it from her then. I was getting older, as most people do, so I decided to shift my focus toward what really mattered, toward something outside myself.

CHAPTER 14:
HOW I DISCOVERED THAT I AM A GENIUS

"We waste so much money on charities when we could be using that money to help people in need."

—*Jeremy Jude*

Joining a charity is much easier than you'd believe; many charitable organizations are so desperate for volunteers, they'd practically let anyone help. I became part of a charitable organization called M.W.A.H., which stood for Meals With a Heart. It was an organization dedicated to taking meals to people's houses, or taking them out to eat, all while having a heart-to-heart with them. As my involvement with M.W.A.H progressed, I was allowed to use a donated large, white van for my routes. Most of the charity's funds were used to pay for food and other expenses for outings with the needy, meaning I got to eat at some of the most upscale restaurants for free. Of course, it's not always a good idea to take a troubled youth to a fancy restaurant. We were kicked out of two restaurants for trying to steal silverware. Both times, the ruffian punks tattled on me, not realizing I was stealing for the charity.

One morning I stepped outside my parents' house with a hot cup of Joseph. (I prefer Joseph to Joe, as it sounds classier.) I relaxed out on my parents' porch watching the sun rise while admiring my charity van in the driveway. I pulled out the company clipboard to see who I was picking up and what we were doing. The clipboard was impractical, though, as I usually decided who to pick up based on what I wanted to do that day.

"Can I tag along?" said a familiar voice. Looking up, I saw a female I had known in my past life—six months and four days ago, to be exact. It was Lana.

"I don't think you want to come along," I said, "I deal mostly with lowlife social deviants." Lana was taken aback by my honesty.

"Should you be referring to them as lowlife social deviants?" she asked. She really didn't understand the charity.

Though it was strictly against company policy, I allowed Lana to come along as a comrade, but I had decided since leaving Italy I would not be making any obvious gestures of love to Lana upon her return. If we were to end up together, it would need to come from Lana's own inner realization that we were soul mates. Instead, I would spend this day showing her the less privileged side of society. She had grown up in a sheltered, wealthy family, so I wanted to show her what my clientele had to endure. She needed to understand that life was not all roses and study abroad trips in Italy with handsome, blonde-haired Italian men whose names were hard to pronounce.

Our first errand was to pick up a fifteen-year-old boy named Travis. When we knocked on his door, he answered groggily in sweatpants and a t-shirt.

"Why aren't you ready?" I asked. He stared vacantly as he scratched his oily scalp.

"Go get dressed. There's a new sushi bar I want to try." I said.

"I can't, man," he complained. "My mom ain't been home since yesterday." Travis had two baby brothers, ages two years old and seven months old; he also had a drug addict for a mother.

"How are the kids?" I asked. He seemed frazzled as he explained that he hadn't a clue how to prepare baby formula; he had been giving them regular milk instead.

Charity is all about humans, and though I really wanted to try that sushi bar, I knew there was always tomorrow or later that afternoon. Lana and I stayed with Travis and his brothers for four hours as we waited on social services to arrive. Lana fed the baby the formula, and I played brain games with the two year old. He was terrible at chess, but he seemed to have a future in checkers until he fell asleep in my arms mid-game. I spent the majority of his nap monitoring his breathing, which became so mundane I fell asleep with him in my arms. Lana woke me up to let me know an intoxicated woman was stumbling up the driveway.

Travis's mother wandered into the house with messy hair and her high heels in hand. Lana immediately took the children to the bedroom, where they remained fast asleep.

"Did you lose weight? You look good!" I said to the mother, faking the compliment; she looked terribly malnourished. I wanted to keep her in a good mood, as from what Travis had told me, she tended to be irritable and obnoxious after she had been drinking. She stumbled into the kitchen mumbling loud nonsense. I ran over and put my hand on her mouth.

"Shhhhhut the hell up! The baby is asleep!" I shouted. Travis's mom ended up falling asleep on the kitchen floor ten minutes later.

An hour later, child services arrived on the scene. After watching Lana explain the situation to them, I said my goodbyes to Travis and the babies, assuring him I would take him to the best steakhouse in town within the week.

As we traveled to our next destination, I hummed along to the sound of the engine. Lana sat quietly beside me as she stared into the distance.

"Do you think they'll be fine?" she asked.

"Yes," I replied.

"How do you know?" she asked, to which I replied, "Because they have the best example of what never to become."

"Where are we going next?" she asked, after several moments of silence between us. We were going to visit an old geezer by the name of Mrs. Adams. She wasn't fun or youthful, but she offered to make me macadamia nut cookies each time I visited her; ours was the epitome of a symbiotic charitable act.

"Damn it!" I exclaimed as we drove past a mortuary. I stopped and got out of the car.

"What is it?" asked Lana.

"These tires..." I shook my head upon noticing the tires were not flat. "Nothing... They're fine," I said as I got back in the car. Lana stared at me as though I were a lunatic.

We arrived at Mrs. Adams's house and knocked on the front door for five minutes. I deduced Mrs. Adams was asleep in her chair, as she often was. I grabbed her key from under the welcome mat and opened the door. Mrs. Adams was in her rocker with her eyes closed.

"Oh, she does this all the time. We should let her sleep for a bit longer," I said. I led Lana to the kitchen where a batch of warm, fresh macadamia nut cookies was non-existent. "Strike one, Mrs. Adams," I muttered under my breath. I really wasn't bothered by the lack of cookies; I just enjoy muttering things under my breath.

After chatting in the kitchen with Lana for an hour, I entered the living room to wake Mrs. Adams up.

"Mrs. Adams, wake up! I want you to meet Lana!" I had to shout because she was hard of hearing. After shouting, I shook her gently, then a little harder, then even harder—perhaps regrettably so.

That's when I knew she was dead; she would have definitely asked me to stop shaking her by then. Lana gasped and covered her eyes like a toddler.

"You've never seen a dead person before?" I asked.

"I have," she said, "but never outside a coffin!" It was ironic, since I'd never seen a dead body *inside* a coffin.

We waited outside for the police; Lana seemed a little shaken, so I non-romantically placed my arm around her. Once the body was removed, I asked Lana if I could read her a poem about our meaningless existence; she asked me not to.

Next on the schedule was to pick up a sixteen-year-old named Jamae. He was my favorite troublemaker to spend time with, as we were very similar to each other. When Lana and I arrived at his house, I honked the horn without coming to a full stop. I kept the van moving at a steady five miles per hour as Jamae burst out the door and sprinted towards the van. I reached back and opened the sliding door. He dove in, and I stomped on the accelerator.

"Did she see us?" I asked.

"Impossible. She's in a deep slumber," he said.

Jamae was a bilingual African-American teenager who spoke both English and Ebonics. I happen to be fluent in Ebonics—among many other languages—but I have translated Jamae's and my conversation into English to help those readers who do not know the language.

"What's going on?" asked Lana. I explained to her that Jamae's mother thought I was a bad influence for taking him to a movie theatre once during school hours. As we spray painted the back of the movie theatre, I quickly realized he was a gifted artist. Once we finished the masterpiece, we rewarded ourselves with a 3D film. Jamae's mom didn't understand that I had been teaching him art. After that incident, I picked him up with the moving-van technique so he could escape from the house quickly.

I drove Lana and Jamae to a Dave & Buster's, which is basically a place where an adult can play arcade games even if they don't bring kids with them. Lana would be needing some fun by now; she still seemed a little tense about the drug addict mother and the rotting old lady corpse.

As we waited for our food, our waitress placed three cups of water on the table.

"How's Freddie?" I asked Lana as I poured four packets of sugar into my water.

"Who?" she replied.

"Your boyfriend, remember? Lana, you forgot your boyfriend's name?"

"Oh, you mean Facundo."

"Sure."

"He's okay I think. He's not my boyfriend any more, though."

I nodded, not surprised in the least. They were doomed from the start; I'll explain why later in the chapter.

Jamae kept staring intently at the arcade section. I told him to go play.

"You misunderstand," he replied, "for by the arcades stands a girl mentioned to you in times past. Her name? Sierra. Oh, what a prepossessing creature indeed!"

Lana and I glanced over to see the girl chatting with three of her friends, accompanied by her mother. She had a voucher in her hand for what I assume was four free combo meals. Lana encouraged Jamae to go talk to her. (Women have a tendency to oversimplify things.) Jamae shook his head, refusing to go over there. His reason was that Sierra was fond of him, but her friends thought he was abnormal.

Lana convinced him to pretend to walk over to a racing game as an excuse to run into Sierra. As we headed over to the girls, Jamae pretended to have a limp.

"Jamae, what the hell are you doing?" I asked.

"It's called a strut, you dullard!" he exclaimed.

"You're the dullard!" I rebutted.

"Shrew man, don't tamper my modus operandi!" he commanded. I was overcome with indignation.

"Watch yourself; I'll bust a hole in your ass!" I shouted, losing myself in the heat of the moment; that's the risk you take when you're a social chamomileon. Poor Lana had to separate us, which brought me back to reality. I apologized to Jamae for my aggression and assured him I would never bust a hole in his ass; Jamae then apologized to me for calling me a shrew man.

After hugging it out, we regrouped and aimed our sights on Sierra. Jamae walked right past her as though he didn't know she existed.

"Jamae, she's right here," I said, pointing him in the right direction.

"Hi, Jamae," said Sierra.

"How do you do?" He asked.

"Just getting food with my girls."

"That sounds like a reasonable plan," he said nervously; I could tell he was off his game. "Sierra, I think it would be of great value if we were to spend time together in the near future." She smiled but, upon hearing the mocking chuckles of her friends, said, "My dad doesn't really want me dating right now." He nodded.

"I comprehend you," he said as he limped away; this time, I fear, he was limping because he was genuinely wounded.

"I'm sorry, Jamae," said Lana as we drove him home. He was in no mood to speak. Lana nudged me to talk to him; I distinctly remember this nudge, as her elbow hit a nerve in my triceps that sent a shock through my entire arm. The last time this happened was when my preschool classmate threw a wooden brick at me that landed solidly on my arm; he lost a clump of hair that day. But this was Lana, so I would not be pulling her hair out.

"If Sierra thinks you're crazy, change who you are for her," I told Jamae.

"No," Lana immediately interjected. "If she likes you, you shouldn't have to change for her or her friends." I shook my head.

"Lana, sorry, but that's the most simple-minded advice I've ever heard expelled from your mouth." We argued back and forth until reaching Jamae's house. I slowed down the van to five miles per hour and told Jamae, "Don't worry about this girl. We'll go to a bar next time." He jumped from the van and sprinted to his house as we sped off.

Lana and I pulled into her parents' driveway, but she didn't seem to be in a hurry to leave.

"Today was interesting," she said.

"Quite," I replied. "Did you know Jamae and Sierra are about the same age as we were when we met?"

"Hmmm…" replied Lana.

There were long periods where neither of us spoke; We didn't know what could be disclosed after all these years of tiptoeing around the subject of us.

"Don't take Jamae to a bar, Jeremy," said Lana, breaking the silence; she was almost always the first to break silences between us. I explained to her that I drank alcohol when I was his age, and it had no negative consequences. Of course, I omitted the story wherein I nearly drowned in an aquarium. Lana reminded me of the time I fractured my spine in Argentina.

"Yes, but that self-destructive drunkenness began because I thought our relationship was over," I blurted out.

"What do you mean?" she asked. I told her about Marco and his fabricated theories about love, which prompted her to ask me about the fateful proposal.

"Did you think I broke up with you in Argentina?" She asked.

"You did break up with me..."

"No, I mean...when you asked me to marry you on the balcony."

"Did you *not* think you'd broken up with me?"

"No, I didn't."

"But you said 'no'..."

"No to the proposal! We were sixteen, and I thought you were high on morphine!"

"I was high on morphine! But that didn't alter the way I felt about you."

"And how did you feel about me?" she asked.

I was honest about my love for her being present since we were sixteen. I was honest about missing her when we were far away from each other. I was honest about her being the only girl I didn't mind giving my full attention to. I was even honest about my animosity towards Freddie. She had captivated me when we met, and I was still her captive years later.

Lana then professed her fears, her pain, and her concerns regarding our relationship thus far. I was in such a state of euphoria at that moment that her brutal honesty felt refreshing; I didn't want to argue with her. In fact, I was so completely under her spell, I nearly agreed with her. Is it love that makes a man stop caring about being faultless? (If not, Lana might have drugged me.) I dare say that I almost wanted to be wrong for once in my life, if it made Lana happy. Just as some delusional dunces pretend to be savants, I could pretend to be meek and erroneous for her sake.

It was 2:04 AM by the time we finished talking, so I drove her home. We said our goodbyes, and off she went into her house. I couldn't sleep that night.

The next morning, I was out on my parents' front porch drinking a hot cup of Joseph, watching the sun rise, mourning the death of the beloved Mrs. Adams. I was irritable due to the dew that had dampened my bottom when I'd sat on the front steps. My meddling mother came out with a coat.

"It's freezing!" she said as she draped the coat over my shoulders. She was no Watson, but I appreciated her attempts at deductive reasoning. I remembered how she had given me a coat in the same way so many years ago, before my first day of driving with Miss Patty and Lana back in high school. My mother kissed me on the cheek and told me she was proud of me.

"It hasn't happened yet," I told her.

"What hasn't?" She asked.

"Never mind, mother."

I watched my mom fetch the mail in her slippers; she had the slightest limp left over from her accident years ago. It amazes me how remnants of near tragedy seem to bring out deep affection in humans. As she walked back towards me she smiled at me warmly; she was always smiling.

"You're a good mother," I told her for the first time in my life. I hadn't said it before now because I had been collecting data on this for years; I wasn't about to make a wild speculation about the quality of motherhood provided by her. She held back tears as she walked back into the house to tell my father what I had said.

"Good morning, Jer," said Lana as she walked up to the house.

"Hi, Lan mower," I replied playfully, to which she smiled. In her hand was a box of her mother's homemade cookies. They were usually mediocre at best.

"My mom wanted you guys to have these," she said, handing me the box.

"Do you know what day it is?" I asked. Friday was her answer, which was technically correct.

"It's October tenth," I replied. She shrugged as though it meant nothing to her. "Nine years ago today was the first day we met," I said as I opened the box of cookies.

I bit into a cookie, put the unexciting cookie down, and pulled a ring from the box. Lana's eyes widened; I got down on one knee and asked her to be my wife. She began to cry, which troubled me until she kissed and embraced me. I lifted her off her feet and kissed her beautiful lips.

My eavesdropping mother came out to see why Lana was kissing me for the first time in years.

"We're getting married!" Lana yelled at my mother. My mother yelled louder than Lana as she embraced us both. My lawyer dad came out upon hearing the shrieks of two loud women.

"They're getting married!" shouted my mother. My dad had one of those man cries as he shook my hand and forced himself to hug me; he was becoming a bit too soft-hearted for a lawyer in his later years.

In a way, I owed this moment to the spider in Colorado. When I left my parents house, I was prepared to forget about Lana forever, and during the first month of hitch-hiking, I nearly succeeded. Had it not been for the spider and his poisonous bite, I might never have come to terms regarding my unquenchable love for Lana. I had fallen into a deep sleep before the search party found me. During that nap, I had a dream. I dreamt that I was William Wallace hallucinating that he was speaking to his dead wife, but then I, William, woke up without her. The vision had a profound effect on me; I felt the devastation Wallace must have felt upon losing his lover, and, I admit, it created in me a desperation to be with Lana again.

I made a promise to myself then that if I lived, I would use my genius mind to get Lana to be my wife. And so, the next evening, I bought a diamond and a ticket to Italy. I then spent the entire flight making a plan to ensure Lana would be my wife.

Purchasing the diamond in Colorado was the easiest part of the plan. The diamond I purchased needed to be set into a ring the size of Lana's finger. To find out her exact ring size, I wrote Lana's parents pretending to be her. It took me a day to master her handwriting, which was a waste of time, as I alternatively typed up a letter. In the letter, I requested they send me the rest of my jewelry, "me" being Lana. The address I gave them was to a flower shop in Florence. The florist was an acquaintance of a family friend that owned the deli shop adjacent to his flower shop. I should have had the jewelry shipped to the deli owner, but I worried about raw meats mixing with the rings.

When I arrived in Italy, I went to the florist to collect the box. He pretended it never arrived until finally revealing that he was joking; I didn't laugh. With the jewelry box in my possession, all I had to do was sort the rings in the box from largest to smallest; There were only three sizes, but I deduced Lana would never own a thumb ring or a pinky ring. The only logical conclusion was that the smallest rings were meant for her digitus medicinalis, also known as the ring finger.

My plan to convince Lana to marry me had to be fail-proof; I needed to be prepared for all possible scenarios, and I was. Here is an excerpt from my forty-seven page plan revealing my preparedness for the unfortunate existence of Freddie:

...and in the unlikely event that Lana has a boyfriend, I must wait for her to return to the United States before proposing; their relationship, of course, must first come to a close. To ensure said boyfriend and Lana do not get engaged or fall deeper in love, I will drop my ring from my pocket in front of Lana at an opportune time. This will likely trigger strong feelings in her, possibly negative, but will ultimately leave her wondering whether or not I was planning to propose to her. With enough emotional baggage to sort through, she won't have time to capitalize on her relationship with unlikely boyfriend...

I admit, I was intimidated the first time I saw Freddie and Lana kissing, but I was put at ease upon discovering what a sweetheart Freddy was. Lana grew up in a nice house with nice parents; she attended a nice private school with nice friends, and ultimately ended up in a very nice university in Italy. As a result, she has always secretly fancied badasses like myself (And by "badasses," I mean uncompromising savants); I credit our relationship in part to her boredom with her quintessential life.

While I suspected Freddie and Lana's relationship would wither on its own, I needed to be sure it was sooner rather than later. Seducing Lana's roommate was just a tactic I used to remind Lana how spontaneous and fun I was; the jealous feelings it may have caused were an unfortunate side effect. I'm a man of honor, integrity, and ethics. To use jealousy as a tool to lure a girl goes against my moral compass; creating a complex scheme to manipulate romantic feelings is far nobler.

The morning we went to the pool at Van Gogh's grandparents'

house, I had placed the diamond ring loosely in my pocket as planned. While preparing to swim, I placed my jeans on the edge of a lounge chair, making sure the diamond ring was susceptible to fall from the pocket's edge. When the ring hit the floor, I knew it would be Lana's instinct to pick it up; I did not know she would hide it from Freddie when he emerged from the house. Still, it was something I decided to use to my advantage.

Lana staying in possession of the ring for the six months she remained in Italy ensured I would remain on her mind once I left. If you recall, she tried to return the ring at the coffee shop. I decided to leave Italy that night for three reasons:

1. I knew hot Sandra and I would have done something regrettable that night.

2. I didn't want Lana to have another chance to return me the ring.

3. Leaving Italy without saying goodbye was pretty badass of me, creating in Lana a more powerful attraction to me.

You may be wondering why Lana didn't hate me for leaving Italy without telling her. In the thank you note I left Freddie, I wrote that I left due to a family emergency; Lana would inevitably find out from Freddie. The only family emergency was that Lana and I were not yet a family of two. It was time to begin the next portion of my plan, laid out in the following excerpt:

> *...and starting a fake charitable organization will inevitably give Lana the impression that I am selfless and generous. The question remains: Where to find children to play the orphans? Even in Hollywood, believable child actors are scarce. NOTE TO SELF: Contact Dakota Fanning to see if she knows any other talented child actors.*

> *We will use the old abandoned building by the creek as the*

orphanage, though I fear it may take some remodeling. NOTE TO SELF: Contact Dakota Fanning to see if she knows of any remodeled abandoned buildings.

While the idea of starting a charity with ulterior motives is repulsive to most, I ask those of you that have started a charity to throw the first stone. Besides, as you may recall, I decided against starting a fake charity; it was far easier to join a real one. I drove that white van five days a week for four and a half months just to prepare for Lana's return.

The week Lana was scheduled to return, I visited her parents. They assumed I was there to casually visit with them. In actuality, I was there to drop subtle hints about my charitable acts; I did so knowing they'd share news of my charitable acts with Lana. There wasn't a day they didn't phone her while she was in Italy; Lana wasn't particularly fond of this tradition, but she was too civil to ignore their call. And since Lana had my engagement ring and many questions for me, I knew she'd eventually decide to ride along with me.

The ride-along was planned as well. I based each of our visits around certain themes that would create in Lana a desperation to get married. The themes were maternity, death, and romance.

I first drove Lana to Travis's house, knowing his mother wouldn't be home when we arrived; I had seen her the night before sitting outside a bar with a tattooed gentleman in an A-shirt. She swayed like the ocean as she handed the brawny man a twenty-dollar bill; he handed her a little baggy filled with poor parenting and regret. The end result was Lana and I taking care of two infants together in a house while waiting on social services to arrive; this brought out Lana's maternal instincts, which often cause a female to start contemplating marriage. You might be wondering why I waited so long to contact social services. There are two reasons:

1.   Travis's house had only become part of my route a week before Lana came along.

2.   Social services had blocked me from calling, as they felt I was essentially "the boy who cried wolf." I know bad parenting when I see it.

With maternity firmly inseminated into Lana's mind, the next step was to create a sense of urgency in her. This brings us to our next theme: death. Before you jump to conclusions, I want to put your mind at ease early on; I did not kill Mrs. Adams. Her death was a genuine surprise to me. I will prove it in this excerpt written by me weeks before Mrs. Adams's passing:

> *...and as we drive to Mrs. Adams's house, I will throw a bag of glass shards on the road ahead in hopes of popping at least one tire. Consequently, the van will come to a grinding halt in front of the mortuary, wherein I will possibly read Lana a tragic poem of our meaningless existence.*
>
> *To seal the deal, we will walk to Mrs. Adams's house where I will ask Mrs. Adams to share stories of her dead husband, whom she loved...*

Things did not go according to plan. As it turns out, it takes more than tiny glass shards to pop a tire. On the upside, Mrs. Adams's unexpected death ended up being far more impacting to Lana's psyche, and even to mine a little. I'm going to miss that old bag of bones, and her macadamia nut cookies.

Jamae's unfortunate experience at Dave & Buster's was also part of my scheme. With Lana feeling maternal and hyper-aware of her inevitable death, I moved on to the romance portion of my plan. The week before this outing, I left a fake voucher for a four-person combo meal in Sierra's locker. You'd be surprised how hard it is to sneak into a public high school. I made the voucher redeemable exclusively on that Thursday, exactly half an hour after we arrived. My planning here was a little sloppy as I didn't check ahead of time to see if Sierra enjoyed Dave & Buster's food or not. The voucher was for four people to ensure Sierra would bring her snobby friends along.

I fully expected Jamae to get rejected by Sierra; she was young and highly susceptible to peer pressure from her friends. Lana witnessing the chemistry between these two teens, and the unfortunate rejection that followed, helped create a parallel between Jamae and myself. He was odd and quirky, and I was a certified genius; We were both, in our own ways, different from most humans. Ultimately, I hoped it would create in her a desire to be with me regardless of my distinct genius mind.

The last step in my plan was to get Lana to share her fears and concerns with me surrounding our relationship; this is why I pretended to invite Jamae to a bar. I knew she would say something about it, sparking a conversation between us. This part of the plan was as important as the rest because I needed to be sure Lana's doubts about me weren't strong enough for her to reject my proposal again. Our conversation that night took a turn for the best; admittedly, that portion wasn't planned.

How did I know Lana would bring me the ring the next morning? In all honesty, I had no way of ensuring that on my own, so I sneaked away to the bathroom at Dave & Buster's and called Lana's mom. I asked her to find my ring amidst Lana's possessions and place it in a drawer Lana opens frequently. At first, she refused to go through Lana's personal belongings; I wished at that moment Lana's mom was one of those mothers with a lack of boundaries and respect for her daughter, though that would mean Lana would have turned out far differently. It was at that point that I had no choice but to reveal that I would be asking her daughter to marry me with that ring. I am relieved to reveal finally that hiding my ring in a box of homemade cookies was Lana's mom's stupid idea. (No offense,

Mrs. Allen, but please be aware your idea was a little stupid.)

You ask how it is that I discovered I am a genius? I will answer your question with multiple questions. Is a genius not creative? Is a genius not persistent? Is a genius not willing to do things our society labels as insanity?

The exact moment I knew I was a genius was when Lana said "I do." An average-minded human could not have ensured that the girl he loved marry him. Furthermore, most humans would never even dream of manipulating circumstances to synthetically kindle the flame of love. I am not like most; I'm wired differently. Am I better than you? No, just different, and that difference happens to give me an edge over most of the population.

I suppose I am a queen ant on this ball-shaped anthill we call earth after all. What's funny is that it doesn't matter; queens are also meaningless. What I failed to mention is that when I poured the syrup over the anthill, even the queen died. With the empty bottle of syrup in my hand, I stood watching the gruesome scene for several minutes, until my wife, Lana, emerged from the house.

"Jeremy, I made us pancakes!"

"That's rather unfortunate timing, love," I said. She stared at the empty bottle and exhaled.

"It's okay, I have a bottle of maple syrup inside," she said as she re-entered the house. I hated maple, but under the circumstances, it would have to do.

As I observed the departed queen ant, laying face down on the syrupy hill, I realized that if I had been that queen staring up at the syrup as it fell from the sky, the only comfort I would have found at that moment was the knowledge that, before the end of my meaningless existence, I had been loved.

If this answer doesn't satisfy you, enrages you, or makes me an outcast in your eyes, I have just acquired further proof of my geniushood (not to mention my invention of the word "geniushood"). The truth is this: Being a genius is not equivalent to being popular, praised, or even acknowledged as a genius. As long as society refuses to acknowledge that I am a genius, I will continue to know that I am one; and if society ever credits me as a certified genius (probably posthumously), it will only serve to confirm what I've known to be true all along:

I am a genius.

ABOUT THE AUTHOR

Jeremy Jude has a degree in Psychology and hopes to one day teach emotional intelligence techniques through his publications.

His comedy influences include Ricky Gervais, Karl Pilkington, Steve Carell, Louie CK, Sacha Baron Cohen, Victor Borge, Jonathan Swift, David A. Adler, Bill Cosby, Andy Kaufman, and Charlie Chaplin.

Jeremy was born and raised in Argentina, where most of his interactions with humans that had mental health problems occurred. This is surprising, considering he worked at a psychiatrist's office in the United States for a year.

To contact Jeremy Jude:
jeremy@scataglini.com